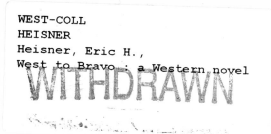

West to Bravo

West to Bravo

A Western Novel

Eric H. Heisner

SKYHORSE PUBLISHING

Skyhorse Publishing books may be purchased in bulk at special discounts for sales promotion, corporate gifts, fund-raising, or educational purposes. Special editions can also be created to specifications. For details, contact the Special Sales Department, Skyhorse Publishing, 307 West 36th Street, 11th Floor, New York, NY 10018 or info@skyhorsepublishing.com.

Skyhorse® and Skyhorse Publishing® are registered trademarks of Skyhorse Publishing, Inc.®, a Delaware corporation.

Visit our website at www.skyhorsepublishing.com.

10 9 8 7 6 5 4 3 2 1

Library of Congress Cataloging-in-Publication Data is available on file.

Cover design by Rain Saukas
Cover photo credit Thinkstock
Illustrations by Al P. Bringas

Print ISBN: 978-1-62914-374-3
Ebook ISBN: 978-1-63220-185-0

Printed in the United States of America

Dedication

This book is dedicated to my family: my daughter who only wants to watch Westerns with John Wayne or papa, my son who is never without his cowboy boots & hat, and most of all to my darling wife who doesn't pretend to understand my obsession for the Western genre but is constantly loving, accepting and supportive of what fuels my passion.

Also to my mom & dad who raised a little cowboy and were always encouraging of his dreams.

Special Thanks

My gratitude goes out to these special folks who helped make this book possible: Amber Word Heisner, Al P. Bringas, Suzanne Zachry Word, Mark Bedor, Dan Farnam & Cory Allyn along with Amy Li, and the experienced staff at Skyhorse Publishing

Author's Tip of the Hat

My profession is Western filmmaker. This novel is a work of historical fiction, but it stands on the shoulders of the classic traditional Western genre in American film.

I wrote this book for the folks I meet at Western festivals and events where a mutual bond is created over the importance of the cowboy in our culture. It is an unspoken brotherhood among those of us who have a westerner within that special place in our soul. There is an everlasting desire in this country for the tales and adventures of the American cowboy. His code of ethics, moral integrity, self-reliance and knowing good from bad, right from wrong seems like an exotic fanciful tale in this ever changing, fast-paced world. A man on a horse inspires us to stop and watch, putting our technological world away for a short moment to see clearly into the basic joy of life.

For me, I have a love for the history of the West. Even more than that, I have a passion for the Western image created by screen legends such as Gary Cooper, James Stewart and the still most recognized star worldwide, John Wayne. From these figures, we as an audience are taught morality tales of characters who experience the violent conflict of man, nature or self and make it through the journey of survival.

I would like to acknowledge the storytellers who have carried on this great tradition. I hope you enjoy experiencing these universal western characters as they breathe new life into a fresh adventure. These unique personalities are of another time in the American West, but belong to us all.

Note about the Illustrations: My good friend, actor, artist and cowboy pal illustrated the wonderfully sketched artwork in this book. His passion for detail and homage to the great cowboy artists is evident in his interpretation of elements from classic western art, masterfully weaving images in to the fabric of our western tale.

West Texas during the American "War Between the States" was a time of isolation and disorder. Men left their homes to fight and their families were moved to safer areas in towns and cities to the east such as Austin and San Antonio. The hardscrabble farms and homesteads cut into the landscapes of the West Texas terrain returned to the earth.

Shortly into the war, federal troops were pulled from the farthest-most posts. The military forts along with vast stretches of the western frontier were left abandoned. Seeing an opportunity and moving in to occupy these vacated positions a short time, the Confederacy was quickly confronted by the realities of an untamed wilderness and native peoples—the Apache.

Chapter 1

The purple sky of sunrise breaks into the dark blue hues of dawn. In the shadows from the rising sun, surrounded by heaving rock formations, a quiet Apache village slowly wakes. Sheltered from the wind, waves of smoke begin to trickle out of the wickiups as the morning fires are stoked to life. The assembly of arched frame wickiup homes covered with branches and woven grass resembles a colony of beehives. Nearby, dozens of horses sleep and lull in the break of day as steam rises from the morning mist warmed from their hides.

The bold, distinct sound of a bugle charge breaks the stillness of the air as the US Cavalry thunders down on the sleeping village. The screams and snorts of horses mix with the clank of sabers and saddle tack. The dust kicked up by running hooves tearing through the settlement quickly consumes the area. Apache families emerge from their homes, and the sharp brutal sounds of gunshots deafen all else.

Running from their dwellings, trying not to be smashed to the ground, barefoot Apache women and children dash through the legs of the Cavalry horses. Apache braves take up arms, slinging arrows and lances at their horseback aggressors. Several wickiups are set to flames as the whole village is consumed in a hazy mass of smoke, fire, and gunshots.

The US Cavalry rips through the village with rifle, pistol, and saber, shooting or slashing everything in sight. Amidst the confusion and carnage, Cavalry horses rise up and buck wildly as soldiers cling to their McClellan saddles and shoot in all directions.

Emerging from a wickiup at the edge of the village, Holton Lang looks out at the annihilation of his village. A half-breed at the middle of his years, Holton wears the headgear of an Apache. His buckskin shirt and leather britches, though, speak more to the tradition of his white forefathers who clung to the higher terrain and lonely mountains.

Born to an Apache mother, Holton was raised with the Apache in the Big Bend region of West Texas until the age of six. His white father, Rawhide Jack Lang, a former mountain man from Colorado, worked as a teamster supplying goods for the military forts. Widely traveled and on friendly terms with most natives, he would visit the Apache villages and bring gifts of blankets and coffee.

When she came of age, full-blood Apache Crow's Wing took a liking to Rawhide Jack. Their seasonal romance was passionate but short lived. When Crow's Wing was killed in a Commanche raid, Holton was taken in by his father. Being a footloose traveling man, he enjoyed seeing a son grow but knew he had not the patience or lifestyle to raise Holton on the road himself.

Stowed at the fort during his father's work expeditions, Holton learned the ways of the United States military at a young age. The summer before his tenth birthday, Rawhide Jack failed to return to the fort. His wagons were found burned on the West Texas plains, but no bodies were found in the area. Maturing to a lean, wiry kid and proficient horseman, the military took Holton in and made a dispatch rider out of him.

With sandy brown hair and deep blue eyes, the racism of his breeding was hardly ever taken as issue, and the ancestral baggage was easy to tote.

After years of being stationed at Fort Davis in West Texas, Holton finally tired of the military life and yearned for a simpler, more peaceful one. Once happening upon the dark-haired Apache woman, Miryan, on a communications run, he was smitten, and the path before him became clear. After twenty years living with the whites and knowing only the ways of the US Cavalry, Holton returned to his native roots and earthen lifestyle.

The sharp, cutting sound of the military bugle call jerks Holton back to attention. He scans the battleground as he shields Miryan, now his wife, protectively. Pushing her back into the doorway of the wickiup, he puts a Sharps rifle to his shoulder. His blue eyes turn to steel as the defense of his family takes precedence. He drops his cheek to the rifle stock— aims and fires—dropping a U.S. Cavalry soldier to the ground. With practiced speed and efficiency, Holton reloads and fires again.

The air is thick with the tinge of black powder smoke and dirt as the Apache pony soldiers engage the U.S. Cavalry. Just as suddenly as they appeared, another bugle call summons the retreat. The sounds of the battle still ring the ears and hang in the air as the blue-coated soldiers disappear in a cloud of settling dust.

Holton stands the same ground outside his wickiup. He takes a long, deep breath and looks around stone-faced at the Apache braves and blue-coated Cavalry soldiers slumped on the ground, dead all around him. He lowers his rifle, looks down at its hot smoking barrel a moment, and drops it to the ground with a quiet thud. Looking back at his wife, they exchange a look of sadness at what the battle and bloodshed will bring. Miryan goes to one of the fallen warriors and begins to sings a death song. Holton looks up to the sky for strength and clenches his jaw as a deep, sad regret fills his eyes.

Chapter 2

A young deer picks and hews at the brush while occasionally perking its head up and looking around wide-eyed. Easing across the rocks and through the brush, Holton and Miryan quietly stalk the young deer. They move unnoticed under a tree and watch their prey. Holton turns to his young wife, and his eyes beam a loving light as they dance over her long black hair. He turns his attention from the hunt and loses himself in his study of her physical form.

Finally, she turns to him and he connects with her kind dark eyes and brings his mind back to the task at hand. She follows his gaze as he motions for them to move ahead. They climb up to a large rock shelf and peer over the edge, getting a better vantage on the innocent deer.

Resting his rifle on the stone ledge before him, Holton pulls the hammer back on the long firearm and pulls Miryan close. He eases the rifle under her arm and wraps himself around her. Settling in to his comfortable hold, Miryan positions herself then takes aim. She breathes in the familiar smell of his sweat and earthen ways. Slowly she peers up at him, and they exchange a longing look that reflects their spiritual connection. For a long while, they forget themselves in each other's gaze while the deer eats, unassuming, in the distance. Holton puts his hand to the firearm and disengages it. Slowly the rifle lowers as he leans in to kiss her.

They come together with a passion that exemplifies the beauty of the peaceful nature around them. Clanking quietly on the stone ledge, the rifle is left to lie alone as Holton and Miryan roll away, entangled in loving embrace. The deer looks up and around and returns to grazing. The shade from the nearby cottonwoods dance on their bodies as the breeze tickles the leaves.

The warmth of midday brings out the dry stone smell of the surrounding rocks and sand as the sun moves overhead. Holton walks into the Apache village with a deer over his mount and Miryan following close behind. They stop near Miryan's family wickiup as an Apache medicine man approaches and blesses the new bounty.

Laying out a well-greased leather hide to cover the ground, several women prepare to dress the meat. Holton sets the deer before them and watches a moment as they cut the skin from the animal while quietly chanting a thank-you to the bountiful spirits of nature.

On the far side of the village, Holton notices many of the young men and warriors gathering near the tribal leader's wickiup. He follows, walking past the ceremonially wrapped slain bodies from the previous day's battle. Pausing before several smaller lifeless forms, he closes his eyes and swallows the painful lump rising in his throat. He looks back to where Miryan stands by the wickiup. For a brief moment, he mulls their lack of fortune in the blessing of offspring.

Chief Yellow Hawk addresses the men gathered before his lodge. His quiet sadness shows behind his time-worn, chiseled features. He rests his hand on a ceremonial lance and looks out to his people.

"The blue jackets gather closer now. They rebuild the house of tall walls and come out to raid and kill our people. Many summers they have lain quiet, and now they grow many dark hands to reach us wherever we make our home."

A tall, strong brave steps from the crowd and raises his hands to the sky. A man hardened by battle, Stalking Wolf has grown restless in the years of peace for the Apache during the war between the Northern and Southern states of America. The hate in his eyes raves as he spits his Apache tongue.

"We need to cut off the hands of the blue jacket! That is the only way for us to make them go away as before."

Holton eases his way to the front of the crowd. He watches as many of the braves rally around Stalking Wolf. He makes eye contact with Chief Yellow Hawk and remains silent to hear the Chief speak.

"We need to make a peace with the Great White Leader. Only then will they stop the hunt on our people. Their numbers are great and their weapons are strong."

Stalking Wolf slams his fist to his chest and yells out for all to hear. "They break the peace. They come here not to steal our horses or food, but to only kill our women and children. You cannot make peace with an animal such as this."

Feeling his loss of power in the situation, Chief Yellow Hawk's eyes become sadder. He pulls himself to his full height and speaks his Apache words in deep, deliberate tongue.

"I have seen the white face come more and more over many years. Now they send the soldier with the hair of the buffalo. The more we fight them, the more they come for us. This is not the way to live. The Apache are strong, but the many years of fighting has taken many of our strongest. Let us settle in peace to make children, teach them our ways, and make a future for our people."

Stalking Wolf steps up to Chief Yellow Hawk and looms over him. He looks like he may strike him down at any moment.

The old man stands strong on his frail frame and watches Stalking Wolf unblinking. Locked in steely gaze, Stalking Wolf hollers with full lungs. "We must fight the buffalo hair and the white face ..."

Stepping forward, Holton draws the attention of the crowd and upstages Stalking Wolf's aggression on the Chief. All the men turn to the tall half-breed outsider who dares to challenge their greatest warrior. Holton speaks with a comfortable familiarity of Apache speech.

"Chief Yellow Hawk is right. We cannot fight the white eyes forever. We must learn to live in peace with him."

Glaring at Holton, Stalking Wolf steps away from the Chief, raises his hands high, and clenches his fists while addressing the gathering. "To kill them is the way to make them leave our homelands. That is what we have done before and must do again."

Holton speaks in slow, deliberate Apache. "No. That was a time, but no more. There is a whole land of white eyes that come across the great blue waters to live a new life. The war with themselves has ended. The blue coats will come back in greater numbers and with them the growers and settlements of people."

Feeling his strength of position returning, Chief Yellow Hawk takes a great breath of air and raises his voice. "Man of Miryan is right. With the blue coats come more white-faced people who cut the land for planting and animals for food."

Infuriated at his lack of influence, with his dander rising up, Stalking Wolf stands before Holton and puffs his chest in defiance. Holton subtly glances around at the many braves rallying behind Stalking Wolf. Knowing his standing in the tribe and feeling the outsider, Holton has overstepped his position before the village.

Putting his face to Holton's, Stalking Wolf nearly spits his words. "You are part white face and a soldier once. Why do they come here to kill us?"

Standing his ground, Holton looks deep into the fiery eyes of Stalking Wolf. "They want to live with no fear. They attack what they do not understand to stay brave."

Stalking Wolf squints and studies Holton for any weakness. "From the early days the white face has killed our people. Our tribe has made no war on them."

"Others have."

"Then we shall join them in war!"

Stalking Wolf pushes men aside and opens his arms to the path of dead bodies ceremoniously laid out. The dozens of bodies consist of men, women, and children. "We will not fear the blue coats or the white face who follow! This is the land of our people, and we will stay brave!"

Letting out a war whoop, Stalking Wolf storms away, followed by many of the young men and warriors. Chief Yellow Hawk takes a deep breath and slowly sags on his aged, bony frame.

"My people, let us not talk of war today. Let us remember the ones we have lost. Go back to your homes and think on a future with peace for our families."

As the crowd begins to disperse, Chief Yellow Hawk walks up to Holton and puts his hand to his shoulder.

"Man of Miryan, I fear I am too old to lead anymore. Stalking Wolf speaks for the fears of today. I can only speak for the hopes of tomorrow."

"You have been a wise man to your people for many years. They will follow you still."

Chief Yellow Hawk looks to the sky for guidance, blinks tears from his eyes, and slowly hangs his head. "I fear they will not." He puts his arm around Holton's shoulder and steers him to his wickiup. "Let us talk of peace."

Chapter 3

Miryan and her mother prepare food around the fire in the center of their wickiup home. The door made of branches and woven grass slowly opens, and the increased flow of air makes the fire jump and crackle. Holton enters, nods to Miryan's mother, and sits nearby. The old woman works slow and steady without looking up. Miryan watches Holton a long moment then turns to her mother. She speaks Apache in a low, quiet voice.

Her mother looks to Holton solemnly, sets aside her food preparation, and crawls over to a leather hide that needs softening work. Gathering the hide and tools in a bundle, her mother stands, nods to Miryan, and steps to the door of the wickiup. She pauses at the door, looks back at the two, then closes it behind her.

Crawling over to her husband's feet, Miryan sits before him. They sit in silence a long while before he speaks.

"Miryan."

"What is to be done?"

Holton peers into her kind, dark eyes and holds them with his.

"With the rebuilding of the fort to the east comes many more soldiers and white face. It is decided that I will talk with the leader of the blue coats."

Trying to remain stoic, Miryan drops from his gaze and puts her hand to his thigh. "You have friends there?"

"I don't know, maybe still." He reaches over and smoothes his hand along her hair and the side of her face. She crumbles into his touch and holds her hands to his.

"I don't want you to go back."

Taking her hands, he puts them to his lap and gives them a gentle squeeze. "Nor do I."

Miryan lovingly caresses his hands in hers. She looks up at him with an interminable love and understanding in her eyes.

"You must."

Holton studies her features as they break with emotion. He slowly nods his head. Clenching his jaw, he watches as a single tear wells up and rolls down her golden cheek. He pulls her close, and she buries her face in his chest and sobs uncontrollably.

The fire crackles and dances as the smoke swirls up through the chimney hole. Holton and Miryan hold each other in tight embrace as they silently say goodbye.

Rising early and walking to the nearby stream, Holton thinks on what needs to be done. He squats on his haunches and tickles the mud with a stick at the water's edge. Silently, he watches birds flit from tree to tree and hop along the ground. The interaction of different varieties of birds completely fascinates and consumes Holton.

The morning sun crests between the mountains and burns bright on the horizon. Tossing the stick away, Holton stands and turns his ear to the wind. Taking a slight sniff, he smells the fires being built up by the women of the village. Holton looks down to his mud-caked boots and thinks of his youth at the military fort. He splashes them off and quietly walks along his back trail.

The air is clear and calm in the mourning village. The dead have been cared for, and now there is a quiet emptiness that hangs over the camp. Miryan leads Holton's horse to the wickiup. The horse is saddled with a lightweight military rig. She receives several crosswise looks as the white man's soldier gear on Indian pony parades through the village.

Holton steps out from the wickiup and places his leather cavalry bags behind the saddle cantle. He slides his Sharps carbine into the saddle boot and ties the leather thongs securing the military-issue bags. He reflects a moment as his eyes study the faded "U.S." stamped on the leather flap of the saddlebags. Turning away from the horse and tack, Holton watches as Miryan exits their home with his age-worn cavalry hat in hand.

They gaze into each other's eyes for a long moment. She steps up, removes his Apache headgear, and tussles the hair on his forehead. With tears in her eyes, she smoothes it back and looks away. He pulls her close and kisses her deeply.

Holton steps away to his horse, puts his hands on the saddle, and stops. Feeling her eyes on his back, he turns around.

"Goodbye, Miryan."

Raising his foot to the stirrup, he mounts and looks down as she offers up his sweat-stained, sand-colored hat reverently. He takes it from her, and they watch one another a long while before he places it on his head. Miryan wipes a tear from her eye and feigns a smile.

"I do not like goodbyes."

"I will do this one favor for Chief Yellow Hawk, and this will be our last goodbye."

He gathers the reins and looks tenderly at his wife.

She whispers in Apache: "We are from the land and together on the land we will remain."

Holton nods and gives his horse a prod.

Everyone in the village watches with a curious interest as Holton rides out. He makes a striking figure as he sits tall in the saddle, clad in buckskins, cavalry hat, and tall boots. Stalking Wolf emerges from his wickiup and follows him with a hateful glare.

Choosing not to take notice of the hostility directed toward him, Holton rides from the village, leaving his Apache family and lifestyle behind.

Chief Yellow Hawk watches as Stalking Wolf moves through the village raising agitation against the white eyes and assembling braves to fight. He retreats to his lodge and sits before the fire. Deep in his being, he feels the age of his years and his soul losing passionate connection with his people. Lighting a pipe to smoke, Yellow Hawk's dark eyes stare into the fire and seem to wither and die into hollowness.

Chapter 4

It is the coldest time of morning as the sun brightens the sky before breaking the horizon. Holton observes the faint vapor of his breath as he squats on his heels and drinks from a leather water bag. He bites off another piece of hard tack and chews slowly while he watches and listens to his horse and the surrounding terrain.

Clenching and flexing his fingers, he wards off the cold and stiffness in his hands. Holton stands and gives a slight shiver to shake off the chill on his buckskins. He finishes the small piece of hard tack and walks to his horse. Putting his hand to its steaming back, he rubs the horse's hide all over to feel for stickers or sore spots.

Satisfied with the soundness of his animal, he takes his saddle blanket from the ground and brushes it clean with his hand. Holton saddles the horse and gathers his gear as the sun peeks over the mountains and begins to chase off the morning dew. With the dawning sun shining brightly to his face, Holton squints as he proceeds east to Fort Davis.

Midday finds the sun beaming hot in a cloudless blue sky. Holton listens to his horse's hooves clamor over rocks and scrub in the West Texas terrain. They continue to ride the seemingly empty landscape, Holton ever watchful of his surroundings. A slight whirl of dust in the distance catches his attention, and he veers his horse to a dip in the terrain near a juniper tree.

Laying low on the horse's neck, Holton eases his hand over the horse's nostrils and whispers quietly in Apache.

"Easy there . . ."

The stillness of the air hangs heavy, and beads of sweat push out from Holton's temple. He watches the ridge nearby as sweat droplets zigzag down his cheek through his whisker stubble and drip from his chin.

Cresting the ridge, six Apache braves travel parallel to Holton's back trail. They ride in loose formation armed for hostility somewhere down the trail. Unmoving, his muscles ache from the stillness as he watches them until they are out of sight.

Finally, taking a relaxed breath, Holton eases his horse out from under cover. He removes his cavalry hat and wipes his forehead on his leather shirtsleeve. Musing to himself, he thumbs the smooth, worn texture of the beaver felt hat. He flicks the decorative acorn on the dirt-covered cavalry cord before placing the hat back on his head.

"Mescalero from the north?"

His horse looks back at him as if seeking approval before giving a full body shake. Holton eases him forward down into a rocky dry riverbed. The sun moves to the west and the daylight burns away as he continues east toward the fort.

Intersecting with the military road, Holton's mount feels their destination near and quickens his step. With the late afternoon sun behind him, Holton spots two sentries monitoring the road to the fort. Not far off, the stockade walls of Fort Davis can be seen, and the smell of campfires and horses hang strong in the breeze.

With quivering nostrils, his mount paws the ground as Holton holds up a moment to contemplate his mission. The horse jerks at the bit and gestures its desire to move on. Flexing his shoulders, Holton adjusts his hat and rides on toward the fort.

The two sentries stand and squint at the seemingly lone rider coming out of the setting sun.

"Halt!" calls out one of the sentries.

"What is your business?" asks the other.

Holton rides up and stops before the two soldiers. With rifles half raised, they look Holton over suspiciously.

"I'm here to speak with your commanding officer about relations with the Apache."

The sentry squints up at Holton and looks over his leather outfit.

"Are you an Apache?"

Holton studies the two men with their rifles cocked and fingers on the trigger. He is alert and cautious to their unsteady nerves and speaks slowly and carefully.

"I have lived with the Mescalero."

Starting to get jumpy and fidgety, Holton's horse eyeballs the second sentry as he slowly circles around to the flank. The soldier before them raises his rifle.

"What do you want here?"

Raising empty palms in a peaceable gesture, Holton glances back at the sentry behind, then looks toward the fort.

"I represent the Yellow Hawk Lodge of the Mescalero Apache. I come to talk of peace."

"We're at war with the Apache."

"Not all Apache."

Suddenly, the sentry at the rear rushes up alongside Holton and tries to pull him from the saddle. Holton strikes out and whirls his mount, sending the sentry spinning to the ground. The other sentry aims his rifle and fires.

A sharp pain runs through Holton's body as the rifle bullet grazes his skull. His horse rears in self-defense, and Holton tumbles backward out of the saddle and hits the ground in a heap. The smell of black powder and the sharp pulsing pain in his head are the last things Holton feels before a swift kick from one of the sentries sends him to a black unconsciousness.

Chapter 5

The sound of poultry and the rustle of stable animals feeding all around open the day as Holton regains consciousness and wakes in a storeroom. He moves to find his hands tied at the wrist in front of him. The act of sitting up sends a pulsing pain through his head that nearly blacks him out again and blurs his vision.

Lounging nearby, a uniform-clad soldier from the fort glances over at the prisoner then returns to a half-asleep state. Dried blood runs down the side of Holton's temple where the rifle bullet grazed him. Holton looks around and grabs his hat. He eases it on to his head, looks out the door, and sees it is early daylight.

"Soldier, I would like to see your commanding officer."

Caught off guard and surprised by the order directed toward him, the fresh soldier jumps to his feet and salutes. He looks around confused and then looks down at Holton in his Native American leather garb.

"You speak American?"

Holton closes his eyes a moment and winces away the pain.

"Who is your commanding officer?"

"Lieutenant Colonel Wesley Merritt."

"Well, you tell your Lieutenant Colonel Merritt that Holton Lang is here to see him. Anyone who served time at this post before the war can vouch for me." A bearded figure clad in fringed buckskins passes the door and glances in as Holton's tone becomes more authoritative.

"Do you hear me, soldier? Now scoot along!"

Bear Benton, a hard man of a rough country, stops and peeks his head into the storeroom. He lets his eyes adjust to the low light and cracks a wide, toothy grin.

"Holton Lang! I thought that was you."

Both Holton and the soldier turn their attention to the doorway.

"Bear?"

Stepping into the room, Bear stretches himself to his full frame in the doorway and leans his rifle on the wall.

"Well bust my buttons, this is about how I figured I'd see you again. How you been?"

Lifting his tied hands, Holton gives them a wriggle. He shrugs as Bear laughs in thunderous amusement.

"Private, cut him loose."

"But, Sir?"

Putting his large paw on the private's shoulder, Bear gives him a shove toward Holton.

"What did you do this time?"

"Just came for a friendly visit with Merritt about relations with Chief Yellow Hawk."

Bear nods and looks Holton over from head to toe.

"They mistook you for full Apache?"

The private cuts the ropes loose from Holton's hands. He looks back at Bear questioningly and steps away.

Holton stands and dusts himself off.

"That's 'bout the jist of it."

"The boys in blue are awful sensitive of late. We lost quite a few recruits in a big encounter south of here a few days ago."

Holton nods and looks out the window at the troopers on the military parade grounds.

"I nearly had my trail cut by several Mescalero from the north."

Bear ambles over and sits on the edge of a table.

"They would be some of 'em. The main body has been raiding hereabouts and being led by a feller called Malfonte. He's been gathering all the Apache lodges together for a big hurrah."

Adjusting his hat over his grazed forehead, Holton looks to his gear on the table where Bear sits.

Looking down, Bear sees a cartridge belt and holster wrapped around an Army .45 caliber revolver. He lifts the bundle and motions it toward Holton.

"This yours?"

Holton gives a nod.

"Thanks."

The soldier looks on, dumbfounded, as Holton takes the gun belt and buckles it on. Bear smiles as he stands and slaps Holton on the shoulder.

"Come on, I'll take you to Merritt."

Not knowing how to handle the situation, the private steps in front of Bear and blocks the doorway.

"Umm, Sir . . ."

Throwing his arm around the private's shoulder, Bear drags him through the door.

"Come along, Private, you may lead the way."

Chapter 6

The clamor of screaming Apache war whoops and the frantic sounds of horses send nervous electricity through the air. Chief Yellow Hawk stands near his wickiup as he looks around dolefully at his unsettled village. The tension is high as Stalking Wolf rallies men around the camp. Women and children move to hiding as the band of Apache braves tear horseback through the village with earsplitting yelps of blood-thirsty song.

The Chief slowly walks among the people and their dwellings. Horses painted for war swerve around Yellow Hawk as they race to assemble for battle. Stopping at the center of the village, the Chief raises his strong but deflated arms and reaches his gnarled fingers to the sky.

He starts a low wailing song that slowly morphs into a strong heart-pounding chant. He begins to pump his arms to the sky and the loose skin on his frail frame rolls and waves like leaves on a distant blowing tree. Women and children gather all around him followed by some of the men. The aggression in the village settles as the old man's chant takes the focus and attention away from Stalking Wolf.

Steering his horse to where the old leader chants and sings, Stalking Wolf rears back and prods his horse closer to the old man, trying to intimidate the fragile chief. Continuing the display without opening his eyes, the aged man gets a surge of energy that compounds his chanting. The entirety of the village assembles around the forceful standoff between the old and young warriors. Stalking Wolf dances his horse around the Chief with a nonverbal threat to stomp him into the ground.

Suddenly Chief Yellow Hawk ceases his dancing, and everything stops and falls deathly silent. With eyes still clenched tightly closed, Yellow Hawk reaches to the sky as if trying to pull himself up to the sun. He stands motionless then breaks into a convulsive shake as he lowers his arms. All eyes and attention is on him as he stands before his people.

Opening his eyes and looking around as if lost for a moment, the old Chief looks up and around at the assembled horseback warriors.

"Do not do this. This is not the way for our people. Stay with your families . . . for if you fight for vengeance, your children will be burned by the sun and scattered to the winds."

His message delivered, Yellow Hawk suddenly slumps to the weight of his long years. He slowly passes the horseback warriors and walks through the crowd back to his lodging. The crowd disperses, and several warriors dismount their ponies and drop their weapons to the ground. The burning rage inside Stalking Wolf burns hotter as he is again compromised in his authority. He sits tall on his pony, and with all his torrid hatred screams to the assembled crowd.

"You will all die like weak dogs whimpering to a white-eyed master!"

He wheels his horse manically and, with a nearly crazed lung-filled war whoop, gathers his remaining warriors.

The village is quiet in justifiable fear as Stalking Wolf and eight braves parade through the camp. Miryan watches as they ride past. Stalking Wolf pauses before her and stares down with a strangely vengeful gaze.

Everyone in camp watches, paralyzed, as Stalking Wolf leads the Apache braves. They ride away and disappear without another sound into the distant wind and dust. Not knowing what to expect if and when they return, Chief Yellow Hawk takes his eyes from the sky and looks to the ground mournfully.

A great sigh escapes him as his eyes glaze over with tears. Slowly looking around at the near destitute situation of his people, he turns away and enters his lonely wickiup.

Chapter 7

Bear escorts Holton across the parade ground epicenter of the fort. Almost as if walking through his childhood memory, Holton recalls the details of his former home.

The stockade and adobe compound at Fort Davis consists of a central arena surrounded by military barracks, stables, and the post general store. He looks to where the livestock corrals are tucked along the south walls with munitions and food storage located primarily behind the Post Store. The multiple rock and adobe structures make up a layout resembling a small village, protected by reinforced adobe walls, four feet thick. Wooden timbers with sharpened point tips protrude from the adobe walls, adding another level of defense.

They walk past an old crumbling adobe structure and turn down a path passing newly constructed military installations. Holton gets his bearings and reminisces about navigating the inside of the fort as a youth. He remembers the military-fashioned buildings lain out on a north/south compass grid that all but enveloped the existing primitive adobe structures.

Bear smiles as he gestures over to several wagons entering the fort by the two main gates. Holton turns his gaze from the nearby third gate for single-file horse traffic. With a nod, Holton acknowledges the wagons and reflects on his past, observing his father's craft of wagon master. There is a long ago, almost forgotten sense of comfort as he thinks of the Fort as a kind of living being. He looks around at the military surroundings in a constant state of disrepair due to the harsh weather elements and the perpetual lack of labor and funding.

Inside one of the larger stone buildings, Holton and Bear are ushered into Lieutenant Colonel Merritt's office followed by the young soldier. Merritt looks up from his desk and studies Holton. There is a twinkle of surprise when he notices that Holton is wearing his sidearm.

He looks to the private who stands near the door nervously, then over at Bear who smiles his never-ending beard-crusted smirk. Knowing Bear for some time, Merritt sums up the situation, lays down his pen, and sits back in his creaky wooden desk chair.

"That is all, Private. Report for regular duty."

The soldier snaps off a salute, which is returned by Merritt. He watches in slight amusement as the private exits with a sigh of relief. Taking a deep breath, Merritt looks up and addresses Bear.

"So, Bear. You can vouch for this man?"

Rubbing his whiskers to hide his smile, Bear gives a small cough.

"Yes, sir. This here is Holton Lang. He used to run dispatch and scout for us back before the war. A better man, who'll keep his hair when things are tight, you'll never find."

Merritt nods and gives a hint of a smile, amused as always with Bear. He wipes his hand across the desk and turns his attention back to Holton. With a sharp, trained military eye, Merritt studies Holton's physical stature and the dark black smear of crusted blood down the side of his face.

"I apologize for the way you have been treated."

Easing his hat back a touch, Holton brushes his fingers just below the bullet graze on his temple.

"It happens."

"That's part of the problem around here. These are mostly all fresh recruits who have no Indian experience. They hear *Apache* or *Comanche* or *Indian* for that matter, and they can't tell the good from the bad."

Bear gives an amused grunt and blurts out. "Hell most of 'em cain't tell between an Indian who wants a blanket or a scalp." Merritt glances over at Bear with a scolding look that surprisingly quiets him for the moment.

Holton nods in agreement. "There are a few bad making the name for 'em all."

Standing, Merritt pushes his chair back and adjusts his coat.

"Yes, I agree."

Holton clears his throat before speaking.

"I would like to talk with you of peace for the Yellow Hawk Lodge of the Mescalero Apache."

Merritt adjusts his chair, pushing it under the desk, and glances down at some reports on his desk.

"What is your relation to them?"

"I live with 'em."

Oblivious to Merritt's apprehension, Bear chimes in.

"How is Miryan?"

Bear turns to Merritt and gives him a broad wink.

"Holton here somehow got himself the most beautiful woman hereabouts. I knew she had a soft spot for him right off. She really . . ."

With a half smile, Holton turns to Bear and gives him a pat on the shoulder.

"She is fine, Bear, you should come out for a visit sometime."

"You got any pups running around?"

"Not yet, Bear."

Merritt seems surprised.

"You have an Indian squaw?"

"I have taken an Apache wife or squaw, whichever you prefer."

Curious, Merritt moves the reports aside and leans forward on his desk. "A white man among the Apache . . . and they permit you to live with them?"

"Family is tough wherever you live."

Merritt smiles and thinks. "They trust you for peace talks?"

Holton nods and takes a moment. "Yellow Hawk is an old friend. The village was attacked by a company of Cavalry several days ago, unprovoked. Many braves along with innocent women and children were killed. We want to come to a peace before the young bucks decide to make war."

Merritt silently listens and looks to his desk. He moves the reports from a pile on the corner to the center of the desk and glances through them. Under a crisp new uniform, Merritt's age and experience still show through.

"We've had problems with an Apache leader by the name of Malfonte. He's been gathering the lodges together. As we try to rebuild this fort, the Indian relations have swelled to the boiling point. We have more settlers moving in and not nearly enough troops to protect everyone."

With reports in hand, Merritt paces behind his desk for a short time while reading. Looking up from the papers, Merritt connects with Holton's gaze.

"I would like to talk peace with you for your lodge."

Holton acknowledges and Merritt turns to Bear.

"Please show Mr. Lang to quarters. Show him a place to clean up and a spare bed for the time he'll be staying with us." Merritt moves around from behind his desk and extends his hand to Holton.

"Mr. Lang, I have some pressing issues to tend to at the moment. Tomorrow we will talk peace with the people of the Yellow Hawk Lodge."

"Thank you, Sir." Holton takes Merritt's hand in a firm handshake. He looks at the sincerity in Merritt's eyes then follows Bear out. Merritt watches them both leave, then looks to the papers in hand again. Silently, his eyes scan the page and he lets out a deep sigh.

"Can peace even exist here . . . ?"

Chapter 8

The afternoon sun finds a mounted column of blue-clad Buffalo Soldiers proudly representing the US Cavalry riding across rolling West Texas terrain. The movement of horse and rider is almost hypnotic as the troopers travel in assembled unison. They are packed light for a week-long patrol with only two supply wagons following. From the light layer of dust powdering their dark blue wool uniforms, it looks as if they have been out for only a few days. Sabers gleam and clank and leather creaks as the troop rides in lines, two abreast. Leading the procession, the swallowtail split red-over-white cavalry guidon flag pops in the wind.

Just over the rise, four Apache braves sit horseback, watching. In the valley beyond the four scouts sit two hundred Apache warriors, painted and poised for battle.

Carrying Holton's saddlebags, Bear leads his old friend into a small adobe and wood-framed room with several canvas-covered wooden cots. He tips his head over to the wash basin in the corner with a mirror above.

Holton looks to the side of the room near the wash basin at a tall, lanky man stretched out on one of the beds.

Twenty-five years Bear's junior, Denny Spreene is a military scout much in the style of the new Cavalry. He is clean cut and lean with civilian clothing offset by high-top boots and reinforced seat cavalry riding britches.

Bear gives Denny's cot a kick as he walks past.

"Hey Den, this here is Holton Lang."

Holton gives a nod, and Bear drops the saddlebags on one of the empty beds.

"The wash basin is over there—get yourself cleaned up." Sorting through a bin, Bear pulls out a hand towel and tosses it to Holton. Grabbing the towel, Holton feels it and gives it a sniff.

"Thanks Bear, washed with soap 'nd all?"

"Only the best for an old friend."

Holton hangs his hat on a wooden wall peg near the bed. "It's good to see a familiar face. Weren't sure if I'd still know anyone here at the fort."

Unbuckling his belt and holster, Holton lays them on the bed next to his saddlebags. He walks to the wash basin and mirror and gives the water a splash. He touches his bloodied forehead with his wet fingertips and winces.

Hanging the towel, Holton scrapes his fingernail at some of the dried blood on his shoulder. With a shrug and a wriggle, he peels off his aged buckskin shirt. Glancing over, Holton notices the scout, Denny, studying him, but pays little attention to his apparent interest.

Denny lifts his head and spits into the corner, missing the spittoon. "I heard of you."

Holton hangs his shirt near the towel and looks down at Denny. "Could be, I don't live no secret."

Lifting his arm, Holton inspects some of the purplish yellow bruises from his encounter with the sentries. He dips the washcloth in the water basin and begins washing. Trying to mask his pain as he stands before the mirror, he feels Denny's eyes prying on him.

Bear pulls a bottle of liquor from the bin and gives the contents a swirl. He pulls the cork and takes a swig.

"Wheeeew . . . that's good medicine! Here ya go, Holton, take a pull of that to fix them wounds."

Holton takes the bottle, tips it back, and swallows a gulp. He winces tenderly and hands the bottle back to Bear. "That stuff'll make you blind."

Bear tucks the bottle back in the bin and coughs. "Kill ya or cure ya."

Watching attentively, Denny spits again, trying to get Holton's attention while still feeling ignored.

"I hear you're a crack shot with a rifle. There are a few hard-to-believe stories that go around about Holton Lang."

Holton glances back slightly at Denny and continues washing.

Plopping down on a cot, Bear leans back against the wall with his hands laced behind his head.

"Ohh Denny, you'd better believe 'em."

Denny gives a skeptical snort toward Bear and looks up to Holton.

"Winchester Arms Company has got a sales agent here to show off their new top-of-the-line rifle that's coming out. The feller is going to have a shoot contest for one of 'em."

From his laid-out position, Denny takes aim with an imaginary rifle. He makes gunshot sounds as he shoots several invisible targets and finishes by aiming at Holton.

"I'm a good shot myself."

Bear gives a guffaw and spits into the can in the corner. "Young Den there fancies himself quite the shooter."

Rising to his elbows on his bed, Denny smiles over at Bear. "I ain't seen none better."

"You ain't seen much kid." Bear gives Holton a wink and smoothes his whiskers. Holton grins and turns back to washing.

Settling back on his bed, Denny puts his hands behind his head and looks over at Holton. He thinks a long moment while watching Holton's back. "You still take up with them savages?"

Wincing at the tenderness of his ribs, Holton doesn't turn to Denny. He pauses a minute then continues nursing himself. "I live with the Apache."

Denny smiles at the prodded response. "You know they're the enemy?"

"Not mine."

Looking over to the corner to spit again, Denny notices Bear taking off his boots while watching the two of them warily. Denny spits and misses, then looks from Bear back to Holton.

"Jest 'cause you have an Indian squaw, that make them alright?"

Bear shakes his head in warning. "Easy does it, Den."

Holton dabs his face with a wet towel as Denny presses on.

"I guess having one of them wild Indian women is like having a good dog."

In an instant, Denny looks up to see Holton's fist come down hard and smash into his face. He takes the punch with a muffled grunt and rolls off the cot onto the floor.

Looking over at Bear, Holton shrugs as he steps back to the wash basin and mirror. Bear sits wide-eyed with the boot he was pulling off still midair.

"I remember you being called Chorradas. You got a bull of a quick temper."

Dabbing the dried blood from his cheek, Holton winces. "He should keep them kind of thoughts to his self."

Slowly recovering, Denny rises from the floor with his nose gushing blood. He grabs his rifle from its scabbard nearby and raises it at Holton. Bear glances up and yells out. "Look out there, Holton!"

Grabbing his buckskin shirt from the wall peg where it hung, Holton swings it at Denny. The leather shirt wraps around the rifle like a whip, and Holton yanks it down and away.

Holton pulls Denny and the rifle toward him, and he greets Denny with a left jab. Holton's fist splashes the free-flowing blood from Denny's already broken nose. Bear winces and lifts his stocking feet to keep them from being stepped on as Denny stumbles back.

"Jeez, Holton . . ."

Releasing the rifle from his shirt, Holton bends over the bed. Denny comes back at him and swings his long arm around to connect with Holton's left temple. Stumbling back, Holton trips on a bed, and Denny is quickly upon him. Fists flying, they stumble back and smash through a table.

The punches are exchanged evenly until Holton begins to tear into a fury, and Denny seems to be getting the worst of it. Locking Denny in a choke-hold on the floor, Holton's eyes go dark and dance with a deadly ferocity. Slapping the floor, Denny's arms flail desperately.

Quickly standing over them, Bear grabs a chair and crashes it down over Holton's back. Holton releases his grip and rolls to the side, and Denny gasps for breath on the floor.

"Sorry, Holton, you'd have killed him."

Slowly sitting up against the wall, Holton nods and looks up at Bear. Rising to an elbow, Denny looks at Holton while Bear squats down on his haunches and grabs them both by the scruff of the neck.

"Now, no hard feelings you two."

Holton and Denny look at each other and back at Bear. Holton takes a deep breath, touches his lip, and spits some blood from his mouth.

"None here."

Bear smiles as he loosens his grip. "Shake hands, you two pig wrestlers."

The two gingerly reach out and shake hands. Holton pains a smile and relaxes with a sigh. Denny wipes away the flow of blood still oozing from his nose.

"No offense intended, Mr. Lang."

Bear helps them to their feet and laughs as he slaps them on the back. He looks at some blood on his hand from one of the two and nonchalantly wipes it on Denny's sleeve.

Holton moves back to the wash basin, refills the water, and starts back to cleaning up. Denny grabs a rag and puts it to his nose to stop the bleeding. He lays down on his bed again and stares at the ceiling.

Watching them go back to almost pre-fight positions, Bear sits back on his bed, laughs, and brushes off his stocking feet. "Good. Now when was that shootin' contest for that special rifle?"

Chapter 9

The parade ground of Fort Davis is a wide open space centered on a flagpole and dressed with lines of rocks in the dirt. Colonel Merritt watches from the officers' quarters and barracks that enclose the area with the main gate directly adjacent.

Soldiers in full blue dress uniform surround the parade grounds in formation. Dozens of men mull about the interior with their rifles under arm or in hand. Cowboys, scouts, and dirt farmers from the surrounding area have all come to Fort Davis for the festivities of the shooting contest.

Mixing with the crowd, Bear and Holton look toward the small platform that serves as a stage. Bear gives Holton a nudge and points to a small stature man in Eastern dude clothes consisting of a derby hat and plaid wool suit.

"He's the feller from the rifle company."

The Winchester man holds a rifle case and walks in peculiar circles while occasionally looking at his watch. His tight little suit and small brimmed derby hat make the man from the East quite the comical picture on the Western frontier. Holton eyes him a long moment and glances over at Bear.

"Looks right at home here, don't he?"

Laughing, Bear rubs his grease-stained leather shirt.

"Yeah, I was gonna ask him where he outfits so I could get one just like it."

They both give a chuckle, and the crowd fills in around them.

The time for the shooting match is near, and the Winchester man clicks his timepiece shut very precisely and clears his voice.

"Excuse me, excuse me . . ."

No one seems to notice as they talk among themselves and mill around. Sitting nearby, Colonel Merritt watches the feeble attempt by the Winchester man to get the crowd's attention and nods to Sergeant Harrison. The sergeant steps to the center of the platform and bellows loudly.

"Attention!"

Everyone stops in midsentence; civilians in their tracks and soldiers snapping to attention while the sergeant addresses the gathered crowd.

"Shooters take the line to the left, aiming to the south. Everyone else, fall in behind."

The crowd jockeys for position, with twenty-two shooters stepping up to the competition line with their rifles. Six infantry sharpshooters march forward from the ranks and fall in at the end of the line.

Sergeant Harrison salutes the assembled shooters and turns to the Winchester man, who stands dumbfounded.

"Thank you, uh . . . Captain?"

The sergeant raises a salute and nudges his uniform sleeve toward the Winchester man, who stares at the stripes confused.

"I'm a sergeant, sir."

"Oh, yes, yes. Thank you, Sergeant."

Sergeant Harrison completes his salute and steps down while the Winchester man clears his throat again and looks out over the attentive crowd. "Well, ladies and gentlemen . . ."

A general snicker erupts from the mostly rugged male crowd. The Winchester man fidgets nervously as he continues on. "I, uh. I am the representative from Winchester Arms Company in New Haven. We are honored to come to the West and to Texas in particular to present you with our newest repeating rifle. We have developed this Special Edition version of the improved Henry with an oversized loop for the gloved hand. We are proud to present it to you today as the ultimate prize for marksmanship."

He turns and picks up the special Winchester from the table. Holding it over his head, the Winchester man displays the new repeater rifle with the egg-shaped lever loop to the crowd.

"Sergeant, if you could please commence the competition."

Sergeant Harrison once again steps to the stage, squares off to the crowd, and bellows to the competitors. "Shooters, toe the line!"

The random pops of gunshots erupt from the last stages of battle between the company of Buffalo Soldiers and the hundreds of warring Apaches. A few remaining soldiers are surrounded by their mounts and dead companions as the Apache rally to attack again. One of the men rises up from behind his dead horse and lifts the red-and-white Cavalry guidon high into the air.

"This is it boys . . . make the United States Cavalry proud!"

As the soldiers hastily reload their sidearm and rifles, a few of the men rally for their final breathing moments. A strange entitlement warms over them as they prepare to die under the flag of their troop alongside their brothers in the heat of battle.

The Apache assemble nearby and rush down from the crest of the hill. The thunder of their ponies' hooves is broken by only the shrill heart-stopping scream of their war cry.

The clear blue skies serve as a backdrop to the U.S. Cavalry guidon as it waves high and proud while the remaining soldiers call out.

"We fight . . . We die!"

"To the last Man!"

"Hoo!"

In the last futile attempt at defense, the Buffalo Soldiers are overrun by the final rush of horseback Apaches. Gunshots split the air, and the haze of black powder smoke hangs heavy over the dead bodies of the brave boys in blue.

The shooting contest continues until it is narrowed down to the finalists. Denny looks to Holton and Private Dedman of the 41st Infantry Company C, who represent the three men selected as the final shooters. They stand at the line, ready for the next round of competition.

The Winchester man stands with his fingers still plugging his ears. "That was some amazing marksmanship, gentlemen. Sergeant, could you please set up for the final round?"

Sergeant Harrison sends several privates down range as he steps to center stage. Rigging is set up for the three finalists at the end of the range with swinging targets. The three men hold their guns close. They run their hands over the hot barrels and rub them down in anticipation.

"Shooters, to their marks!"

Denny, Holton, and Private Dedman step forward, stand at the shooting line, and ready their rifles.

"Start the targets!"

The targets are set in motion as everyone clears down range.

"Fire!"

The three finalists each shoot seven rounds of ammunition from their rifles in quick succession.

The blood-soaked Apache war screams echo across the valley as the guns and clothing are pulled from the dead troopers. Hundreds of Apache warriors ravage the dead and dying of their material earthly possessions.

The guidon for the company of U.S. Cavalry hangs limp across the prone body of an officer's dying horse. The military beast heaves his last short breath under the saddle as its wide white eyes slowly relax and roll back. The horrific carnage of the battlefield is a mass of dead animals and human bodies; Apache warrior and military soldier, side by side.

Chapter 10

The afternoon sun burns brightly just over the pointed stockade walls of the fort. The long sharp shadows cut through the crowd assembled before the stage on the parade grounds. Denny, Holton, and Private Dedman are positioned near the front of the crowd as the final shooting tallies are made.

The Winchester man finally turns to the crowd, and, in his funny and quirky way, again holds up the special prize rifle.

"The winner of the Special Edition Winchester is . . ."

Denny looks around. beaming, and takes a step toward the platform as the Winchester man calls out.

"Holton Lang!"

With his jaw slack, Denny looks shocked and embarrassed. Bear laughs loudly and gives Holton a hearty slap on the back.

"Good shootin', you lead slinger! Now you can buy everyone a drink."

Shaking hands with several of the fellas around him, Holton takes the compliments. Denny looks back at Holton with genuine surprise as his ego deflates.

"But, I . . ."

"Excuse me, Den, musta got lucky 'nd hit 'em all dead on."

Holton moves past Denny and steps up on the platform. The Winchester man studies Holton's worn leather shirt and Western style, then excitedly and hands him the rifle.

"Congratulations!"

Taking the rifle in hand, Holton studies the details of the oiled walnut stock, oversized loop, and case-hardened frame with side loader gate. He works the lever several times and takes aim at a point beyond the stockade walls. Satisfied with the feel of the rifle, Holton lowers it and smiles to the crowd.

Curiously, he holds the rifle in one hand and swings the stock out and the barrel toward himself in a twirl-cock sweeping motion of the large loop rifle.

Amused, the crowd gives up a cheer, and Holton looks admiringly down at the firearm.

"This will do."

The Winchester man stands wide eyed in amazement of the lean, leather-clad frontiersman. Holton tucks the rifle under his arm and tips his hat to the gun agent. Bear steps up a few stairs to the platform and turns to the crowd. "Who'll have the first honor of buying this man a drink? Drinks all around at the General Store!"

The crowd whips into raucous howling and cheering, then moves en mass across the parade grounds to the General Store. As Holton reaches the bottom of the stairs, Bear grabs him around the shoulders and escorts him to the gathering celebration.

Inside the General Store, past the trade stock, a tasting room is set up in the back with a bar and a few mismatched tables and chairs. Holton stands at the thick plank bar that sits atop several large whiskey barrels. He lays the new Winchester down across the rough-hewn wooden planks and raises a mug of beer to his lips. Everyone gathers around to get a closer look at the special edition rifle and its large lever loop.

Private Dedman eases along the bar with his drink and looks over the rifle. He gives a low whistle and smiles.

"Nice shooting, Mr. Lang. I's a marksman from when I was a kid. Ain't never better shootin' than today. Suppose it made me some nervous to have all of 'em watchin'."

"Thanks, Private. A man's nerves will affect the outcome."

Bear pushes his way through with a beer in one hand and a large shot glass of whiskey in the other. "Holton here's got nerves of steel. I've seen him in a running fight afoot and horseback loading and firing without breaking stride."

Reaching out and smoothing his hand over the fine finish of the big loop rifle, Holton smiles. "I suppose it'll be a lot easier with my new repeater rifle."

Everyone laughs as Holton finishes his drink, and a soldier hands him another. "Here you go, Lang, don't want ya to get dry!"

At the end of the bar, Denny looks on and drinks straight from a squat ceramic jug of whiskey. He walks over and leans in to Holton. His liquor breath is tinged with the copper smell of blood from the fight earlier in the day. "Hey, Holton, I'd like to see you shoot like that again."

Holton glances over his shoulder at Denny. "Don't need to."

Laughing, Bear cuts between the two before it turns to fisticuffs again and gives another roaring toast.

The small room gets louder and seems ready to bust at the seams as the drinks go around. One of the soldiers from New Orleans, Private Bellows, jumps up and seats himself on the plank bar top. He takes off his union blue kepi, sets it aside, and picks up the special Winchester rifle. Aiming it around at the roof rafters and various oil lamps, he beams with excitement. "Hey, Mista Holton, how was it you twirled this here fancy long-arm?"

Switching his beer mug to his left hand, Holton takes a swig and gives the motion of spin-cocking the rifle with his right. "You just kick 'er out and back to ya then bring it around."

The room erupts again in cheering as Holton raises his drink in toast to the rifle and takes another swig.

Beaming with excitement, Bellows leans out from the bar top and swings the rifle out and toward himself. With a tooth-breaking *crack*, the end of the rifle barrel smashes Bellows in the mouth, and the whole room drops silent and winces. Spitting teeth chips and blood, Bellows sits bleary eyed and stunned.

Bear grabs the Winchester rifle before it hits the ground, and Bellows falls back on the bar in painful shock. Looking down at him, Bear looks in as Bellows opens his mouth to reveal his busted front teeth. "Oooh, best leave it to the professionals."

Bear slaps the rifle down on the bar in front of Denny and helps several soldiers remove Private Bellows from the bar.

Looking down at the rifle in front of him, Denny's eyes run green with envy. He reaches out and grabs Holton by the shoulder. "How about you sell me that rifle?"

Peering down at Denny's scraped knuckled paw on his shoulder, Holton gives a sly grin.

"Why Den, that would almost be dishonest."

He shakes Denny's hand from his shoulder and watches as they try to get Private Bellows on his feet. Holton picks up the special Winchester from the bar top and turns to Bellows, who is mercifully set in a nearby chair. Bellows licks his lips and continues to spit blood into a pail. He feels around in his mouth with his finger and looks like he might break down and cry.

"Gol' damn, I think I done broke three teeth."

"Sorry 'bout them choppers, Private."

Holton takes a step back from the crowd. With a tin beer mug in one hand and the new Winchester in the other, he gives the rifle another twirl-cock. Everyone chuckles, amused as Bellows takes a swig of whiskey and spits another stream of blood into the bucket.

The front door to the General Store suddenly bursts open, and a body stumbles in a few steps and falls flat. Behind him, two of the soldiers on guard at the fort's entry gate stand dumbfounded. One of the guards steps forward and gestures to the fallen man.

"He said he had to come here first . . ."

Private Dedman pushes through the crowd and turns the man over. "It's Morrison."

Holton looks to Bear questioningly. "Mitchell Morrison?"

"Yeah, he was out with a company on patrol."

They rush over to the body on the floor and look down on the old Indian fighter. He lies limp in Private Dedman's arms with several bloody arrow stubs in his side and one each on his back and arm. With a flicker of life, Morrison opens his eyes and looks up at the men surrounding him.

"Get me a drink . . ."

One of the soldiers peers over Bear's shoulder. "We need to get him to medical."

With heaving breaths, Morrison tries to talk. ". . . it was a massacre."

Bear takes a knee and leans in, resting his hand on Morrison's cheek. He eases his own glass of whiskey to Morrison's lips. "Mitch, it's me, Bear. How many were there?"

Morrison rolls his eyes to Bear and strains to stay conscious. As the whiskey hits bottom, a slight smile of gratitude surfaces before he turns grim.

"There were hundreds. Malfonte has all the Apache lodges riding together."

"How many others are with ya? Who survived?"

With the slightest of movement, Morrison shakes his head to the negative and blinks tears from his eyes. "I wanted to stay . . . someone had to warn the fort . . . the Apache will wipe out all the territory."

In a pained final breath, Morrison's hand falls from Bear's arm, and his eyes roll back. Slowly, Morrison's body falls limp as he finally joins his fallen comrades in battle. The only sound in the once raucous room is the scuffling of boots on the rough wooden floor and mourning sighs as the crowd holds quiet.

Chapter 11

Late in the night, oil lamps illuminate Colonel Merritt's office as several of his officers stand around his desk. Keeping to the rear in the dark corner of the room, Holton and Bear look on and listen during the proceedings. Merritt finishes speaking and moves to the large territorial map of West Texas on the wall. He motions Bear over, waits for him to move forward, and steps aside. "Bear, show us where you think this conflict happened."

Stepping up to the large map, Bear traces his finger from the location of the fort to terrain in the north and west. "The company was on patrol through here. . . . They were only out a few days when attacked, so they must have been about in this area." His finger circles a large area on the map, and Merritt steps back and leans in closer.

"Now where does that put this large force of Apache?"

Moving his finger slightly to the south, Bear taps the map. "Morrison said there were hundreds that came down on them. For that to happen undetected, they would have had to be positioned in this area. From there, they could swoop down and wipe out anything in their path."

Crossing his arms, Merritt looks to his officers and rubs the gray beard whiskers under his chin. "Do we think Malfonte can hold together a hostile force that large?"

The room is silent as the officers look to each other nervous and unsure. Bear scratches his boot toe on the floor and looks up to Colonel Merritt.

"Could be. They got the taste now for blood and revenge. Ain't gonna stop till there's more spilt on the ground. Got all of our patrol supplies, too."

Back in the corner, from the shadows of the room, Holton's eyes blaze at the map and the location of the Apache war party. His face seems to be etched in stone as all emotion is void.

Colonel Merritt stands behind his desk at full attention and addresses the officers. "I want this fort locked down. No one is to come in or out without my specific permission, friendly or not, until we know more about the position of this hostile threat. Is that understood?"

A general nod in agreement puts the officers at attention.

"Alright then, pass the order on, and we'll send out scouts at first light. Put on an extra guard unit at the ready."

Merritt salutes and dismisses the officers. He looks to Bear and Holton. "I'm gonna need you to get your best scouts together and find out what is going on out there."

"Yes, Sir."

Merritt looks to Holton for a moment and receives no acknowledgment. He looks back to Bear and waves a salute. "That's all."

Grabbing Holton by his arm, Bear shuffles him out the door into the dark night.

Saddling his horse, Holton slides his new rifle into the scabbard and ties on his old Sharps behind the cantle on top of his blanket roll. He checks his cinch and looks over to Bear, who stands watching.

"They ain't gonna let you leave without a fight."

"Am I gonna get one from you?"

"Nope."

"Thanks, Bear." Holton untethers his mount and leads him out of the corral. Stepping out of Holton's path, Bear pushes his hat back on his head to scratch his mop of hair.

"Say hello to Miryan for me. I'll be sure you make it through the gate."

With a nod, Holton mounts his horse and eases him along as Bear follows.

The parade grounds are nearly dark with the exception of a few oil lamps illuminating the barracks and the light of the moon. The night air is broken by the quiet *clop, clop* of a horse's hooves. Coming across the parade ground, Holton rides into the light, and Bear gives him a pat on the leg as he peels off and disappears into the shadows.

Several soldiers on foot approach Holton and his mount with their rifles at the ready. Sergeant Harrison steps to the front of the pack and addresses Holton.

"Mr. Lang, we have strict orders not to let anyone leave this fort."

Holton rides past him, on toward the front gates. "Mine ears are still ringin' from the shootin' contest, Sergeant, can't hear a thing you're saying."

"Mr. Lang. We cannot permit you to leave."

At the fort gates, Bear slips up to the sentry and presses a Bowie knife against his mid-section.

"I don't want to hear a word of argument. This Bowie will have you cut in half before you yell out."

"Yes, Sir."

"Now, let's ease open that gate so we can have a peek outside."

The sentry lifts the bolt and opens one side of the double door.

Watching Holton ride past, Sergeant Harrison stops his men, and they stand at the ready.

"Halt, Mr. Lang! I don't want to have to shoot you."

Holton looks back over his shoulder. "You have your duty and I'll see to mine. I recommend you save any fight you got for the Apache which are a' comin'."

Turning his back on the soldiers, Holton gives his horse a jab. He trots across the parade grounds and slips out the front gate unmolested. Sergeant Harrison stands dumbfounded as the sound of Holton's horse fades into the distance outside the fort walls.

"Damn! Who opened that gate?"

Followed by the soldiers, Sergeant Harrison runs to the front gate just as the sentry pulls it closed. The clank and rattle of the soldiers running stop as the sentry lowers the bolt, securing the door.

"Who authorized you to open that gate?"

The Sentry steps back and motions toward Bear. Sergeant Harrison turns to Bear, who sits in the shadows, calmly smoking his pipe.

"We are under strict orders that no one leaves these walls!"

"Holton comes and goes as he pleases."

"We could have stopped him."

Bear takes a puff of the pipe, which lights up his face. He shakes his head slowly.

"No . . . no, you couldn't have."

Chapter 12

The first rays of sunshine crown the horizon and gleam on Holton's back as he rides through the West Texas terrain. The worn and sweat-stained buckskin across his shoulders shows a golden patina as the uneven fringe bounces in the morning light. He pauses momentarily to study the tracks and trail on the ground, then spurs on. The grim look of his features and the set of his jaw tell the news of the venomous trail he follows.

Smeared with war paint and blood, Stalking Wolf and five braves return to the village of Chief Yellow Hawk. They ride with many fresh scalps hanging from their war ponies. The dried blood takes on a blackish color over the fleshy side of the scalps. The short curled hair of the Buffalo Soldier hangs alongside the straight locks of the white officers.

The six horseback braves ride dusty circles around the wickiup of Chief Yellow Hawk. They give a piercing war whoop that raises the old chief along with the attention of the whole village. Stalking Wolf yells in Apache for all to hear.

"You that call yourself Yellow Hawk of the Mescalero Apache, show yourself!"

Coming from the farthest corners, the village begins to assemble. Yellow Hawk steps from his dwelling and looks up at Stalking Wolf with age-worn eyes. He stands transfixed in distant memories as he studies the fresh scalps on the war lance for a long while.

Stalking Wolf glares down at Chief Yellow Hawk and raises his bloody trophies to the sky.

"We have avenged the murderers of our people!"

Chief Yellow Hawk looks wearily around at the amassing crowd. He puts his hand out and touches Stalking Wolf's horse. Pulling from his inner calm, he tries to settle the nervous mount. He looks around at his people and speaks up to Stalking Wolf.

"You have put your people to slow death with your actions. The more you make war on the Blue Coat, the more they will hunt us, kill our children, and destroy our food."

Shaking the scalps and waving them over his head, Stalking Wolf pulls his horse away from the calming influence of the Chief and tries to rile up the crowd.

"The Apache is strong. We will not be weak, but kill the Blue Coat Pony Soldier!"

Riding his horse through the crowd, Stalking Wolf pushes the scalps in the faces of the onlookers. Chief Yellow Hawk speaks out to all the people.

"We have made a peace with the white leader. You cannot stay here with blood on your hands, Stalking Wolf. Take your war prize, take your bloodlust, and leave this place."

Insulted at the mention of not having his place in the village, Stalking Wolf looks down angrily at Chief Yellow Hawk.

"These are my people! The great, Apache war leader Malfonte will avenge the many wrongs of the white eyes. I will not leave, I will lead!"

Raising his arms, Chief Yellow Hawk looks to the sky and closes his eyes.

"Go back to your homes, my people. Choose to live in peace. Follow not this warrior who chooses a dying war over lasting life in peace." He begins to sing in a slow wail, and the crowd disperses and returns to their dwellings.

Watching helplessly as his influence dwindles, Stalking Wolf becomes infuriated. He lets go a screaming war whoop and rides his agitated horse in a manic circle. As the dust rises, his braves back off to a safe distance from the display.

Suddenly, Stalking Wolf ceases his tantrum and rides up beside Yellow Hawk, who chants with eyes closed and arms raised high. With a threatening motion of his lance, he raises it above the Apache leader. The dispersing crowd momentarily stops and turns. Opening his eyes, Chief Yellow Hawk continues to sing unafraid, and Stalking Wolf screams out.

In a ferocious fit of rage, Stalking Wolf plunges his lance into Yellow Hawk's chest and lets out a bloodthirsty war whoop. Staring down from horseback, he glares around at the horror-struck village.

Dropping to his knees, Yellow Hawk clutches the lance that pierces his body and stares up at Stalking Wolf. Slowly, he looks down to the ground where his blood is beginning to pool in the dirt and shakes his head sadly.

"Go now, you have killed us . . ."

Yellow Hawk crumples to the ground, and his squaws run to his side. Everyone stares in quiet disbelief as Stalking Wolf watches, momentarily motionless. He finally wheels his horse around and rides away through the village.

Returning to the Apache village, Miryan holds a basket of gathered food. She sees the gathering and watches the commotion near Chief Yellow Hawk's wickiup. Sensing bad spirits in the air, Miryan slowly walks toward her wickiup while still watching the crowd in the distance. Suddenly the crowd disperses with a scream. A man on horseback, painted for war, rides quickly toward her, followed by five similarly painted braves.

Stalking Wolf slides his mount to a stop and rears his horse in front of Miryan, knocking her over. Their eyes connect for a quick moment, and she recognizes his deep-set hatred for all whites, including her husband, burning in his dark soul. She climbs to her feet and tries to run.

Stalking Wolf's horse nearly tramples her as he reaches down and grabs her by the arm. Dropping her basket, Miryan fights wildly as Stalking Wolf pulls her to his horse. She gouges at his eyes and punches at his groin.

The braves circle to watch the flailing tigress of a squaw. With heavy blows, Stalking Wolf clubs Miryan with his fist until she stops struggling and finally falls limp. He looks up at his braves and his bloodshot eyes flare with violence and hate.

"We will not fear any white face! I will take what is his. Man of Miryan will feel the pain of his people's war on us."

A blood-curdling war yelp is heard across the village as Stalking Wolf and his braves ride away to the north. At the edge of the Apache village, Miryan's handwoven basket lies quietly upset in the rocks and brush.

Chapter 13

The following day, Holton rides into the village of his adopted family and sees a people wrapped in mourning. The low wail of a Death Song draws him to Chief Yellow Hawk's wickiup. Holton scans the eerily depressed surroundings and steps from his horse. Taking a moment to gather his emotions, Holton stands before the Chief's home, pulls the animal skin door aside, and enters.

Inside, the body of Chief Yellow Hawk is laid out and prepared for ceremonial burial. Holton drops to his knees and looks up at Rain Pony, one of Yellow Hawk's squaws. "What has happened here?"

Rain Pony looks up sadly at Holton and feigns a smile through her mourning. "You were at home with our people. He cared for you and loved you like a son."

"And I for him. How did this come?"

Looking away with fear and sadness in her eyes, Rain Pony talks in low tones with eyes to the ground.

"Stalking Wolf ended his life and has joined with Malfonte of the Mescalero to the north. Yellow Hawk wishes you peace to come someday."

Holton takes a deep breath as the anger toward Stalking Wolf wells up inside him. He looks to Rain Pony and the other squaws. They avoid eye contact as he stands before them.

"There will be no peace for some time. Many tribes have joined to make a great war."

"Peace for you was his parting wish."

A strange moment passes as Rain Pony avoids speaking the thoughts that pass through her. Holton feels the anxiety and scans the other squaws for a clue to her behavior. Once friendly to him, all of Yellow Hawk's squaws turn their eyes away and try not to connect with Holton. Suddenly his eyes flare and a pain emotes from his whole being.

"Miryan?" Holton's heart sinks as the utterance of his wife's name brings tears and sobs to the squaws of Yellow Hawk. With his jaw clenched to keep from screaming out, he turns and exits the wickiup. He leaps onto his horse and rides hard across the village. Swinging down from the saddle at Miryan's wickiup, Holton slowly staggers to the door and enters.

It seems that all of nature hangs deathly still while the native village sits under a quiet cloud of sorrow.

Chapter 14

Horse hooves clop through the water of a small creek as Holton scans both sides for a sign. His eyes suddenly lock on several rocks along the bank with their moss side turned over. Riding up the embankment, he reaches the top of the ridge and looks out over an empty landscape.

With blind determination, Holton tracks Stalking Wolf and his braves over barren flats and rocky terrain, day and night. With the distraught look of an animal on the hunt for survival, he presses on without sustenance or sleep.

The night is dark with only a sliver of moon to break the shadows. A small fire illuminates Stalking Wolf and his five braves in their camp. The Apache brave, Choking Wren, turns and stares uncomfortably into the darkness. He listens intently as he watches, then looks over at the small female form lying nearby, curled in a protective ball.

"What will happen when Man of Miryan comes for her?"

Standing, Stalking Wolf walks around the campfire and looms over the body of Miryan. He leans down, studying her, and watches the rise and fall of her shoulder as she takes scarce breaths.

"She may die yet. We will not leave her here. When we join the Mescalero to the north, they will take her and do with her what they want."

"But what of him?"

Stalking Wolf looks up and glares at Choking Wren.

"You stay here to meet him if you fear him following."

The braves all look around at each other anxiously. Choking Wren watches their reluctance and looks again to the black night.

"I will not wait for him alone."

"You fear his white blood?"

"No, I fear his Indian part."

Circling the braves, Stalking Wolf walks around and scowls down at each of them. He spits his hateful words as they remain in their lounging positions. "I could have killed him many times before. If he comes to us, he will be blind in agony. He will be an easy kill."

Choking Wren looks up at Stalking Wolf and meets his gaze. "A wounded mountain cat is most dangerous. There is nothing easy with Man of Miryan."

Stalking Wolf looks away and out into the dark night. The lines on his face show anger and hatred, but his eyes show fear.

The campfire turns to embers and dies down as the Apache braves settle in for sleep. At the edge of the firelight, Holton's face appears briefly illuminated as he moves silently through the brush.

In the early hours of the morning, before sunrise, Holton creeps into the renegade camp. In the dim light, he crawls forward on his belly like a snake without making a sound. Sliding his knife from his belt, he eases up next to a sleeping Apache brave.

Facing the sky in peaceful slumber, the warrior's eyelids twitch as Holton puts his knife to the throat of the sleeping man. He quickly and quietly presses down, slicing the brave's neck through to the bone of the spine. The dying man's eyes spring open from reflex and his lungs gasp for air through cut windpipes while blowing blood.

Holton slides around the first body as the life blood drains out and eases up to another sleeping Apache lying on his side. Thrusting his blade up into the base of the slumbering man's skull, Holton holds the Apache's mouth and twists the knife until the body movements slow.

Moving slow and quiet, Holton creeps over to the next Apache victim. Out of the corner of his eye, he sees the body of Miryan roll over. Tears well up in his eyes and a short gasp escapes his lips. "Miryan . . ."

The Apache beneath him wakes as if death had whispered in his ear. Holton grabs him quickly and thrusts his knife into him repeatedly. The muffled screams of the dying Apache wake Stalking Wolf and the other two braves instantly.

The camp becomes a flurry of motion as Holton charges across the fire circle and lunges at Stalking Wolf. Holton's knife cuts deep into his nemesis's face, and Stalking Wolf screams in agonizing pain. In a flash, the other Apache braves leap on Holton and thrust their knives into the fray.

Broken apart temporarily, Holton faces off with Stalking Wolf and the two Apache. One of the braves steps back and pulls the blanket covering Miryan. He raises his knife to kill her, and Holton quickly throws his blade. The knife whirls through the air and buries itself deep in the Apache's skull just above the nose.

Not waiting for the Apache to hit the ground, Holton leaps at Stalking Wolf and tears into him, tooth and nail. The remaining Apache brings his knife down in Holton's back and pulls him from Stalking Wolf. Holton turns on him and attacks furiously. Briefly out of the fight, Stalking Wolf wipes the blood from the flowing gash on his face and turns to flee.

Wrestling the Apache brave into a choking hold, Holton sees Stalking Wolf heading for the ponies. Full of rage, he reasserts himself with a manic fury and twists the Apache's head until it breaks in a gruesome crunch and the body falls limp.

Jumping to the back of one of the Indian ponies, Stalking Wolf looks back momentarily before riding away into the darkness. Frozen in his tracks and watching for what seems a rage-filled eternity, Holton finally turns to Miryan.

The adrenaline still pulsing through his veins, Holton takes staggering steps toward his wife. He drops to his knees and crawls to her side. "Miryan, I'm here . . ."

He wraps his arms around Miryan, embraces her, and whispers. "We are of the land . . . together on the land we remain."

Blood-smeared and injured, Holton holds Miryan in his arms. The sun peeks over the horizon and rises on the ravaged camp. The early rays of a new day shine down on five finally dead Apache warriors who lie in an unceremonious circle surrounding the reunited couple.

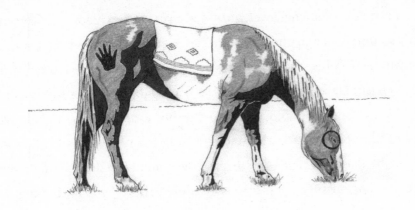

Chapter 15

A burial ceremony commences as the Yellow Hawk lodge of the Mescalero Apache honor their chief. His age-worn and lifeless body is laid out by his remaining squaws on display for all. The air is filled with mournful singing and wailing that echoes through the depressed village.

Company C of the Ninth Cavalry rides out of Fort Davis. The troop is led by Bear Benton, in frontier shirt and military britches, and several Indian scouts. The double-file line of horseback troopers parades abreast and looks glorious in their ranks. They ride to their soldier duty with the hard look of determination for avenging their fallen military brethren.

Buzzards circle and pause to swoop down for inspection of the several unmoving human forms strewn about. Unattended, Holton's horse wanders into camp and congregates by the other Indian ponies still tied. They chew on the sparse grass and brush and occasionally watch the large scavenger birds as they dive in and hop across ground between the dead bodies.

Holton sits hunched over with Miryan cradled in his arms. He wakes and squints through the dried and crust-hardened blood on his face. Slowly he rolls his shoulder and winces at the pain of the knife wound in his back. He adjusts Miryan in his arms and gently rises to his feet.

Pained and slow, he walks to his horse and eases Miryan over the saddle. Holton stops and takes a long moment to push away the cloud of darkness that tries to pass over him. He slips his foot into the stirrup and swings up into the saddle behind Miryan, pulling her close. Touching his heels to the horse's flanks, they slowly ride from the camp, leaving behind the horrendous stench of death all around. The gathering buzzards patiently glide in wide aerial circles until all is still again. Finally they swoop in to clean the desert of the rotting, sun-bloated debris.

The Apache village once lead by Chief Yellow Hawk is nearly abandoned. Until recently a thriving community, the dwellings now appear hollow and empty, stripped of their essence of home. The last of Yellow Hawk's tribe packs their families and belongings on travois to leave. Fear in the eyes of the people seems to be the driving motivation for leaving a once-contented communal site. Beaten trails of foot and pack animal lead in all directions as the tribe, without leadership, is scattered to the wind.

Out on an empty high plateau, the cool desert air of evening sets in as Holton breaks thin sticks for a fire. The small smokeless flames rise and dance around the larger branches as the fire takes hold. He warms his hands and looks over at his wife, curled on the ground nearby. Jaw clenched, he watches as her breath comes faint and slow. The aching from Holton's wounds begins to stiffens as the crusted blood shows black in the firelight.

Holton lies on the ground next to Miryan and pulls her close. He watches the fire lick around the sticks as he caresses her long, dark hair. The flames flicker and glisten in his eyes as tears form and slowly find their way zigzagging down his face. Tucking his head into her body, he grips her tight and weeps.

The chill of night sets in as the warmth of one body comforts the other into the afterlife.

Chapter 16

A lone horseback rider crests a ridge and looks over onto hundreds of Apache camped down below. He watches the encampment for a long time while studying it. Finally, turning and looking at his back trail to the south, Stalking Wolf feels confident with his deliverance. A gaping, bloody gash crosses Stalking Wolf's face, which accentuates his dark, hate-filled eyes. The wound will someday heal to a raised, jagged scar and a constant reminder to be forever scanning for the one following in his trail. He looks again to the gathering below and sneers faintly. Jabbing his heels into his mount, he glances once more behind him before riding down toward the Apache stronghold.

Company C of the Ninth Cavalry rides through an Apache village of empty wickiups. The troopers ride in formation and look eerily around at the abandoned dwellings. Approaching the head of the column, one of the native scouts nods and motions to the Chief of Scouts, Bear.

Recognizing a strange look on this stoic scout's features, Bear veers from the group and follows the Indian as he sniffs the air questioningly. The scout leads toward the far edge of the encampment and glances over his shoulder at Bear. His hand on his rifle, pulling back the hammer, the scout speaks in a low quiet voice. "Village not empty,"

The two meander through the empty dwellings and ride to a wickiup just past the others. Bear pulls his carbine rifle from its saddle scabbard and looks around cautiously. The native scout points with his own rifle toward the seemingly abandoned home. Bear slides off his horse and drops the reins to the ground. He moves over to the dwelling and touches the animal hide covering the entry. Looking up at the scout again, Bear gives another sniff as the scout mumbles Apache and covers his nostrils and mouth. "Death."

Carefully, Bear pulls back the door to the wickiup and peeks inside. Adjusting his eyes to the darkness and the single beam of light from the hole in the roof, Bear scans the room. Toward the back of the dwelling lies a curled-up human body. Bear pushes the door back, tosses it aside for more light, and steps inside. "Halloo . . . you there?"

He holds his rifle ready and cautiously approaches. Standing over the body, he suddenly lowers his rifle and kneels beside the form. "Holton?"

Bear leans down and looks closer to see his old friend clinging to the edge of life. Holton is in bad shape with blood still seeping from black, crusted wounds. Bear smells the air again and winces at the coppery smell of blood and a slowly dying man. He gently touches Holton and rolls him over.

With a weak moan and shallow breath, Holton startles and opens his eyes faintly.

"Miryan . . ."

Bear nods and pats Holton's shoulder. "I know pard . . . I know."

Chapter 17

The Mescalero Apache dance around the many campfires singing songs of war. Their long shadows reach up from the pulsing firelight, their forms playing out into the night with their dance across the starry sky.

A pioneer wagon train snakes through the desert, cutting through the landscape of red rocks and towering sandstone buttes. The red dust kicked up by the horses and mules swirls around the wagons like an ever-clinging sandstorm.

Inside one of the wagons, Holton wakes to find himself laid out atop boxes of gear and mercantile supplies. He looks around stiffly while wincing at the soreness of his wounds.

"Hello?" He lifts his head painfully. "Where am I, 'nd who's driving this rig?"

The wagon creaks and rocks as Holton tries to twist his body so he can see to the front. He finally struggles to one elbow and pushes some folded canvas aside. Peering over a supply box, he sees the silhouette of a familiar hat and shoulders.

Bear swivels in his seat and gives that familiar broad grin, bearded and toothy.

"Hiya Holton, ya ol' sharp-shooter. Warn't sure whether you was going to make it or not."

Holton winces as the rocking of the wagon pains his wounds. "Make it where? What's going on?"

Roaring with a hearty laugh, Bear turns forward again and gives the reins a slap. Talking over his shoulder, he drives on. "Well, we had a nice group of wagons pass through the Fort headed for California, so I bought us a share and signed on."

Holton winces and closes his eyes a moment. Chasing the pain away, he takes a deep breath. "Where are we now?"

"Arizona Territory."

Taking in the information, Holton blinks his vision clear and studies the boxes of supply goods that surround him. "Who's stuff is all this?"

Bear hollers at the team, then turns and looks over his shoulder. "What's that?"

"What is all this stuff?"

"It's half yours."

"How'd that happen?"

"Figured you didn't need two rifles so I sold your old Sharps 'nd a few other things and bought some trade goods."

"To trade for what?"

"Whatever we might need up in Prescott."

Lifting the canvas side flap, Holton peers out through the swirling dust. He can see several wagons to the front and rear as they snake through the valley.

"You said the wagons were going to California?"

"Yep, that's the idea."

"Ain't Prescott in northern Arizona?"

"Yep."

"What?"

Bear glances back at Holton with a look of caring concern. "I know a feller east of Prescott who's got a ranch. If he's still around, he's gettin' on in the years and could probably use the help. Beautiful place with a butte across the way and a creek down in the valley."

Holton lowers the flap and lies down. "Alright, that's enough. I don't want to hear anymore."

Laughing, Bear slaps the reins again. "Good, you should rest up. Sit back, enjoy the ride 'nd relax."

Giving the reins another slap, Bear stands in the box and hollers at the team. Holton closes his eyes, lets out a deep breath, and tries to relax into the rocking jolt of the wagon.

The wagons are all circled for the evening. Holton sits with Bear while they both eat from tin plates. He looks around at the diverse mix of families and frontiersmen headed for California. Holton carefully scrapes the remaining food from his plate and slowly takes a bite. Chewing awhile, he swallows painfully and looks over toward Bear.

"Why did you bring me along?"

"Half this stuff is yours."

Holton shakes his head, irritated, and Bear stops smiling.

Lowering his plate and finishing chewing his mouthful, Bear takes on a serious tone as he looks up at Holton. "You were near dead . . . naw, you were well past that. Maybe better t'a say t'was near alive."

"Why didn't ya jest leave me be?"

Studying Holton a long while, Bear seems hurt. He bristles at the mention of him abandoning his friend to let him die. Bear rubs his eye with a quick brush and gives a huff of breath.

"You and me don't have many friends we can count on. We have to take care of the ones we got. No one else at that there fort would have taken as good a care of ya."

Putting his plate aside, Holton looks around. "Could be I didn't want to go away."

Bear raises his plate again and continues eating. He looks to Holton occasionally, but mostly talks between his chewing. "Back there, your head was full of death and hate. You would have let yerself die or got yourself killed along with who knows what. Them Apache are on the warpath, and the last thing anyone needed was an old ex-dispatch rider scout heading up his own vengeance trail."

Bear takes another bite of food and thinks a minute. "Figured the best thing for ya was to git you out of the territory and git ya livin' life somewheres else. There was nothin' left for yous but pain and sufferin' back there."

Lying back against the wagon wheel, Holton puts his plate aside and watches Bear finish eating a second helping. He tilts his head back and looks up at the evening sky. The wisps of cloud pass overhead, and he breathes in the possibility of a new life before him.

The morning sun breaks the early light of day as the wagon train makes camp along the old military road through Tonto Indian territory. Holton helps Bear harness the team and hitch up the wagon. To the south, a dust cloud of a single horseback rider approaches and catches their attention.

Bear smoothes the reins along the animals' backs and rubs his whiskers.

"Sure kicking up some dust. Wonder what that's about?"

They watch as the rider draws up on the wagon train and talks to the wagon master. The two have a discussion, then turn their attentions and look over in Bear and Holton's direction.

Turning away and giving the rump of his mule a slap, Bear moves around to the other side.

"Hey Holton, look away now, or they might be thinking we're interested."

Holton continues dressing the team while the rider and wagon master trot over. Bear stops what he's doing and spits a long stream of tobacco to the ground. The two riders stop, and the wagon master leans down to rest his elbow on his saddle horn.

"Hallo there, Bear."

"What's kickin'?"

"This here is Hennricks." The wagon master motions to the rider next to him, and Bear gives an informal salute.

"Hennricks says there's a stagecoach depot jest to the south of here a few miles. They get regular supplies and are interested in selling and trading some."

Bear digs his wet quid of tobacco out from his lip and tosses it to the side. He wipes his fingers on his shirt front and spits.

"That's fine, that's fine. Why ya telling us?"

"I don't want to redirect the whole wagon train down there cause it'll cost a few days, and I'd like to get through this Tonto range. If'n you'd take a wagon and a few riders, it would save us a lot of time and get enough supplies to last us through."

Holton leans on the wagon and listens to Bear's exchange with the wagon master. With nary a glance at Holton, Bear extends his hand to the wagon master.

"Sure, we'll do it."

"Good, I'll round up some riders to go with you and gather the supplies list."

They shake hands, and the wagon master and rider peel off down the wagon train. Holton steps away from his position on the wagon and stands next to Bear as they watch the wagon master talking to each family. With a sharp jab of his elbow, Holton punches Bear in the ribs. "Now I don't mind a' goin', and I don't dislike gettin' supplies and breakin' from this snail trail, but I'm gettin' a little tired of being volunteered."

Giving a grunt, Bear holds his side and shrugs. "You don't have to go."

"I'm a' going, but I'd appreciate it from now on, you'd leave my volunteering to me."

Bear smiles and rubs his side. He gives a grunt as he goes back to harnessing the team.

"Yes, Sir. Feelin' better are ya?"

Chapter 18

The wagon train weaves between the buttes and mesas of the Arizona desert. Three horseback riders follow the wagon master as he trots up next to Bear's wagon. He rides up alongside and sees Holton sitting next to Bear on the bench driver's box. With a paper list in his hand and a small metal box in his lap, the wagon master reaches over from the saddle toward them. He puts a hand to the side of Bear's wagon and keeps pace with his own mount.

"Here's the list of accouters."

Holton takes the paper and looks it over. The wagon master squares himself in the saddle and motions back to the three riders behind him. "The fellas here will ride with ya." Holding out the metal box, he gives it a rattle. "This is the monies put in to cover the supplies."

Taking the tin and opening it, Holton looks over to the wagon master. "You have it counted?"

"Yep, jest keep a tally sheet. Hennricks will lead the way."

Closing the tin, Holton tucks it in the back of the wagon behind the driver box. The wagon master gives a casual salute and steers his horse back among the other wagons.

Looking back at the riders following and Hennricks to the south ready to lead the way, Holton turns to Bear. "You all set, Bear?"

Bear stands and gives the reins a slap. "Hot footed 'nd rarin' to go!" Veering off from the wagon train, Bear's wagon follows Hennricks and the two escort riders.

Following a sandy cut in the desert, Bear's supply wagon moves along with one rider in the lead and the others following. Holton gives Bear's leg a tap and motions to the Indian pony tracks cutting their trail.

"Yep, I seen 'em."

"They ain't taking much care to hide 'em."

The wagon rolls on, and Holton and Bear carefully scrutinize the landscape. Holton casually lays his rifle across his lap and thumbs a few cartridges into the side gate, filling the magazine. Without looking overly watchful, they scan the area for any hostile actions. The dust and heat start to bear down on them as the wagon churns through the soft terrain.

Suddenly, with only a subtle turn of his head, Holton's eye catches something. He carefully studies the thick brush and low-hanging trees passing on the wagon's peripheral. The lack of movement and stillness raises the hairs on the back of his neck. He raises his thumb to the hammer on his rifle and eases it back with a click. Bear glances over at the distinct sound and grips the reins a little tighter.

In front of them riding in the lead, Hennricks turns and motions ahead. Suddenly he jolts and spins from the saddle with two arrows stuck in him. Bear slaps the reins as Holton snaps off a shot into the brush and levers his new Winchester. He lowers the rifle as he scans the brush for a target.

"Which way?"

Bear looks around and hollers, "Hell if I know . . . jest out of here!"

Jerking the rifle to his shoulder and letting a round go, Holton drops an Indian rider behind a palo verde tree. He levers the rifle again and snaps off another shot. The wagon moves out, and several arrows tear into the canvas just behind the driver's bench. Bear looks behind him as the thud of arrows stab into the wagon. Holton continues to lever his rifle and shoot.

"Go! Go . . ."

Bear stands in the drivers' box and slaps reins again as the team snorts, digs in, and starts to kick up some dust.

The two escort riders come up from behind with guns ready. They ride alongside Bear and look to him questioningly. He slaps the reins again and bellows to the escort riders, "The stage depot must be just ahead. Go on and tell 'em we're coming in hot!"

One of the rider's mounts steps sideways, rears, and kicks out as the two riders pull away and move ahead. They ride onward at a hard gallop until an arrow slices through the neck of one of the riders, dropping him to the ground. The other rider looks back at the wagon and Bear waves him on franticly.

Holton fires repeatedly into the thick underbrush as the wagon churns on. "Get us out of this scrub, Bear."

Bear gives Holton a cynical look as Holton feeds more cartridges into the rifle's magazine. Holton looks up at Bear then quickly raises the rifle again and fires a shot.

With a holler and shake of his head, Bear pushes the team hard through the loose rocky ground. The wagon wheels throw up clouds of dust and grit as they cut through the desert sand. One wheel smashes into a large rock in the trail and Holton is nearly thrown from the wagon. He swings out with his arm and holds tight with one hand while nearly dropping his rifle. "Watch where you're going!"

"Damn the rocks! Hold on!"

Arrows whiz through the air, and suddenly, one of the horses in the team drops to his knees. The other horses' eyes roll white in wide-eyed panic and charges in the opposite direction. With the rattle and crack of the rigging, the wagon jackknifes and rolls over, sending Holton and Bear sailing through the air into the desert vegetation.

Coming up with rifle in hand, Holton runs to Bear and kneels down beside him. He sends a few more shots into the brush and pulls Bear to his feet. "No time for a siesta. Come on, ya lazy bastard."

Bear spits dirt from his teeth and scoops his pistol from the ground. The two dash, while firing their guns, through the scrubby underbrush toward the stagecoach depot ahead.

Running at the adobe building, Bear and Holton see the black powder smoke and hear the bark of guns through the cross-cut porthole windows. They dive for cover, and Bear turns to Holton as he begins to reload his pistol. "I hope they ain't in that cabin shooting at us."

"Let's not give 'em much of a chance. Move it!"

The two run up to the adobe building and press their backs against the wall. They fire their guns toward movement in the brush as they dash around toward the front door.

Several arrows bounce off the outpost, and the dry adobe walls splinter with bullet hits. Holton stops at the front doors and pulls cartridges from his belt to reload his Winchester. Bear pounds on the thick wooden doors and bellows, "Let us in!"

The doors open a crack, and Bear slides in, followed by Holton. An arrow sticks in the door and it quickly closes again, followed by the slamming of the wooden bolting brace.

Inside the station building, the only light comes from oil lamps and the small rays of light coming through the gun-port shutters. Bear and Holton let their eyes adjust for a moment then look around. Cochran, the depot manager, sights his rifle through the window and patiently waits for his shot.

The depot manager's wife, Mrs. Cochran, pulls Bear and Holton away from the door and sits them down. "No extra holes or sticks in ya?"

Bear smiles and looks to Holton. "No, Ma'am. He always looks like that."

Holton looks to a Mexican man, Sancho, who steadily loads the rifles and pistols on the table. "Pardon, Señor. Any forty-four center fire cartridges?"

Without looking up, Sancho slides a box toward Holton and continues ramming lead in the cylinder of a Navy pistol.

Jeff Ryan, the remaining rider from the wagon train stands by a window nervously. He watches Holton a second then peers out the window. Holton breaks open the box of cartridges and fills his rifle. "How many do you see out there?"

Cochran snaps off a shot and shuffles to another window. "They're sticking close to the brush, so it's hard to get a good count of 'em." He fires another shot and moves to the next window. "From what I saw of you's coming in, there are two less."

Watching the windows and moving across the room, Bear peeks through one of the gun ports. "How about that wagon?"

Firing again, Cochran shuffles to another window. "It's clear for now. If'n we don't get it in before dark, it'll be picked clean by mornin'."

Scrambling to yet another window, Cochran grabs a whiskey jug on the way. He takes a long swig before looking around and catching Mrs. Cochran giving him a scolding glance. "Yer team is loose and a'wandering by our corrals. We should pull them in too 'fore dark or them Injuns will eat 'em."

Bear moves to another window and looks out. "Hey, them's a good team!"

"Them Tontos will steal anything a'hoof. If they don't ride 'em, they eat 'em."

Holton steps up to one of the unoccupied windows and looks out. Ryan comes up behind him and leans on the wall. "What about them other two out there?"

"They're dead."

"Are you sure?"

Holton aims his rifle through the gun ports. He takes a long breath and nods remorsefully. Squinting, Holton waits then fires his shot. Ryan looks away, pained, and turns to Bear at the next window.

"We have to get back to the wagon train in case they're attacked. I've got family there to protect."

Bear snaps off a shot with his pistol and shakes his head.

"We ain't going anywheres for awhile kid."

Pulling his rifle in from the cross-cut gun port in the window, Holton peers out to study the area surrounding the upset wagon.

"We'll get that wagon righted up, pull the team in, and head out at first light tomorrow."

Ryan turns to Holton and pleads.

"Tomorrow? We should be heading there now."

Continuing his watch from the window, Holton shakes his head. "You'll be of no use to your family being dead."

Holton puts the rifle to his shoulder and takes slow, deliberate aim. Ryan stands close and looks out. "You see one?"

"Maybe . . ."

Ryan watches impatiently and tries to see over Holton's shoulder. Bear carefully pulls Ryan away and whispers to him, "Step back boy, don't crowd 'em. Ya gotta give a man some breathin' room when he's about to kill another man."

Beads of sweat trickle down Holton's cheek as he watches unblinking. He squeezes off a shot and steps away from the window. Ryan steps in and looks out.

"You get 'em?"

"He won't bother us no more."

Watching through another window, Cochran coughs. "They're heading out. I can see the dust of six, maybe seven of 'em riding out."

Heading over toward the door, Bear stands with his pistol ready. "Let's get that wagon righted and pulled in. Might be one of their tricks. Could be they'll circle back in a while."

Cochran steals another swig from the jug and sets it aside. "Sancho, help them fellers with their rig."

Sancho puts down a rifle and grumbles under his breath in Spanish. "Why do I always have to go out when there is danger?"

Bear slips out the door headed for the upset wagon followed by Holton, Ryan, and Sancho.

Chapter 19

The wagon train slowly circles and makes camp for the night. The sun sets and fills the sky with brilliant orange, purple, and yellow streaks. On the distant ridge, silhouettes of Indians on horseback assemble and watch the display of wagons.

Looking up to the ridge, the wagon master studies the figures. His hard features show no hint of feeling, but his eyes speak of experience. Urging his horse on, he rides to each wagon and relays a cautious warning.

Oil lamps glow from inside the stagecoach station. In the shadows of the porch, Holton and Bear peer out into the darkness. Bear sends a stream of tobacco spittle out past the wood planks. "What do you reckon we should do?"

Holton listens to the night then glances at Bear. "Those Injuns we tangled with was just a small part of a large mustering."

Bear nods and curls his bottom lip whiskers up to his mouth. "I saw the tracks. Figure they were heading toward the wagons?"

"Yep."

Bear gestures to the inside the depot and speaks quietly.

"That Ryan kid is itchin' to git back to his family. He'll be hard to hold back."

"We'll keep 'em here till morning."

Bear scratches himself and sits quietly, thinking. The question on his mind is that of any man who sits at the crossroads of fate. Looking over at Holton, he gives a slight snort. "Will three of us make the difference?"

Leaning forward, putting his elbows to his knees, Holton interlaces his fingers. He looks out at the dark moon shadows and bows his head uncertain. "Could be . . . but not likely."

"We still goin'?"

Holton glances over and exchanges a look with Bear. "You can do whatever you have a notion to do."

Standing, Holton glances up to the dark night sky. He gives Bear a pat on the shoulder as he turns to go inside. Bear looks up at him and grunts. "We'll most likely be killed."

"Everybody gets dead someday. Rather it be in the saddle than a rockin' chair."

Bear looks down at the rocking chair he sits in. With a shrug, Bear gets up and follows Holton inside. The heavy wooden door closes, and the bolt slides into place.

Illuminated by lantern glow, Cochran looks up from packing his pipe and wipes his hand on his britches. "Any sign out there?"

Bear settles into an old creaky chair by the fireplace. "Nary a soul. Couldn't be any more peaceful."

Still pacing the floor, Jeff Ryan holds his rifle tight. "Maybe we should head out now since they're gone."

Bear watches as Holton throws his leg over a stool and turns to face Ryan.

"We'll head out in the early light of morning. No use taking chances at night."

"What about the wagon train?"

Mrs. Cochran places a plate of food in front of Holton then steps back to the cook pot. Holton looks over at Ryan and stirs the hot food on his plate.

"They'll hold tight till we get there." Taking a bite, Holton chews then turns from Ryan's continued pacing to Mrs. Cochran. "Ma'am, you're a good cook, mighty tasty."

Smiling, Mrs. Cochran turns to her husband. He takes the pipe from his teeth and spits. He gives his chin a wipe and nods toward her, returning the smile. "A woman ought to be a good biscuit roller, a fair shot, and a warm body to make it out here long."

Bear laughs and takes a plate. "Holton there is quite the cook his self, if'n ya like Injun food 'nd such."

They settle in with their food and slowly eat to the loud pop and crackle of the fire. Mr. Cochran puffs on his pipe and gazes into the curling flames.

Still peering out the gun ports, Ryan looks around anxiously. "I think we ought to get out now."

Holding his fork midway to his mouth, Holton pauses and looks to Bear. He slowly lowers his fork to the plate and leans into the wooden table with both elbows. He looks toward Ryan and speaks slowly and deliberately.

"I told you twice already. There ain't gonna be a third. If you want to throw your only good chance away, you can do what you want to do."

Bear finishes chewing and fills his fork again. He shovels his mouth full as he speaks.

"Ah, there's nothing better than a meal after a fight. We'll have much better odds of reaching them alive in daylight."

Holding a plate out to Ryan, Mrs. Cochran lures him to the table. "They're right, son. Have something to eat. There's nothing that can be done tonight."

Grudgingly accepting the plate, Ryan sits next to Holton as he continues eating the meal. He picks at the food and stares at the plate despondently.

Holton glances over at Ryan then looks up to Bear, who answers with a shrug and continues eating. Holton turns back to his plate, trying to think of some words of encouragement for Ryan. With nothing honest or comforting coming to mind, he remains silent and continues eating.

Circled around several campfires, the wagon train is forted up for the night. Several of the men stand near the wagon perimeter with rifles slung in their arms. Everyone speaks in quiet whispers as they listen to the strange sounds coming from the darkness. The unnerving echoes of coyote yelps are answered by the hoot of an owl, and the men quietly stare at each other while holding their firearms at the ready.

Playing cards across the table, Bear studies the back of Cochran's hand. The two grizzled men look comical in the efforts of concentration furrowing their brows. They make a noisy pair as they alternate between Bear spitting and Cochran sucking his pipe.

Mrs. Cochran washes up the table around the card game. She watches as Holton lies down on the floor with his pistol belt and rifle nearby. Bear looks over and sees Holton wince painfully as he settles in.

"How them wounds treating you, Holton?"

"They're holding up. Jest tired."

Peering out the gun-port shutters again, Jeff Ryan stares into the dark night. He looks at Holton and Bear then back outside.

"I think we ought to go now."

Putting his hat over his eyes, Holton takes a deep breath and gives a slight shake of his head. Several deep breaths later, Holton is asleep and snoring quietly.

Bear shuffles the cards and watches as Ryan finally gives up the watch. The young man settles in against the wall, lowers his head saying a silent prayer for his family, and waits for morning.

Chapter 20

The morning light eases into the valley surrounding the wagon circle. Weary bodies shift from guard duties as others rise from their sleep. A coyote howls, and suddenly a shrill, terrified scream shivers through the camp.

Rushing to the perimeters of the wagon circle, the sight of two mutilated bodies lashed to the ground with rawhide ties causes some to drop their firearms and wretch in horror. The gruesome figures stripped of their skin seem to be Hennricks and the other supply rider.

The wagon master steps up and signals two men to recover the bodies. With blankets ready, the two men rush from the security of the wagons to cover the mutilated beings. In a heart-wrenching cry, Hennricks gives off a wailing moan as the wool blanket touches his raw, flesh-torn body. The man over him stumbles back and vomits at the sight of the tortured man.

Screams from the womenfolk are muffled as they are quickly pulled away from the horrific sight. Several men step outside the wagon circle and hesitantly approach the still breathing figure. They stand and stare, disbelieving their eyes and the human body's endurance for survival.

Suddenly an arrow whizzes from the brush and one of the men arches forward with an arrow deep in his chest. Quickly tossing a blanket over the other supply rider, the men make a quick dash back to the wagon circle. Rifles are raised and several shots are thrown blindly out into the surrounding brush.

The alarm of "*Indians!*" is yelled across the camp.

Standing quiet and peaceful, the stagecoach depot blends into its colorless desert surroundings. Sancho moves inside as Holton, Bear, and Ryan step out to the porch. Bear fills his chest with air and puffs it out. "A fine mornin'."

Bear deflates as Holton jabs him with his elbow and nods toward the horizon several miles to the north. A small trickle of smoke drifts skyward. Holton glances at Ryan carrying his saddle and observes that he hasn't yet noticed the darkened sky. "Ryan, go ahead 'nd load your gear in the wagon."

Waiting until Ryan steps away, Bear looks up to the smoke again. "Suppose it's the wagon train?"

"Yep."

"How do you want to play this, pard?"

Looking to the wagon and the torn tarp hanging to the flexible ribs of the awning, Holton scratches and tugs the hair at the nape of his neck. "We'll all ride the wagon from shooting positions. Would be best to keep Ryan from horseback, or he'll charge in and git himself killed."

They exchange glances then step from the porch, moving toward the wagon and Ryan saddling his horse. Spitting a stream of tobacco juice, Bear wipes his whiskers and grunts.

"That'll give us as good a play as any."

The wagon circle sits prey at the bottom of the small valley. A dust cloud whirls around the wagons as Indians ride their horses in a galloping ring around the perimeter. Shots are exchanged from both parties as the Indians hang from the side of their painted war ponies and shoot over the withers.

Small fires can be seen through the rising dust as an occasional flame-tipped arrow arches from the brush and stabs into a victim or wagon. The choking smell of gunfire is the only comfort to the defending settlers. A canvas wagon cover along the fighting perimeter bursts into flames after a fire arrow pierces through it. Women and children toss shovels and handfuls of sand on the fire while the men continue to shoot and reload.

The loose teams of livestock jump and skitter around the center of the defensive circle fearfully as the occasional arrow falls among them. In the midst of the confusion, women gather the small children in a huddle at a protected area to avoid being trampled or shot. The ear-piercing war screams of the native attackers send the cold chill of panic throughout the camp. Battling men and women steadily load and fire their guns, knowing they are fighting for survival and the lives of their families.

Leaving the stagecoach depot, the supply wagon is hitched and moving with two saddled horses tied on behind. The canvas is rolled back, giving a clear view through the partly broken ribs of the wagon. With boxes and bags of supplies piled around the edge, there is some measure of defense for a shooter in the wagon bed.

Sitting up front next to Bear, Holton looks back at their young companion sitting with rifle ready. He exchanges a look with Ryan and feels sympathy for his fear of familial loss. The wagon rolls forward in a thrust of momentum as Bear urges the team on.

Mr. and Mrs. Cochran stand off the porch of the adobe stagecoach depot and wave goodbye. "Good luck to y'all."

They watch the supply wagon roll out into the desert and scan the distant sky nervously. The small plume of smoke continues to tickle the breeze in the north just over the path taken. Mr. Cochran sucks at his pipe and shakes his head. "Well, we'll never see them again. Best stick close to the cabin for a few days, Mother."

Mrs. Cochran nods, and her features sadden, watching them leave. "Tis a' shame to have them go."

He reaches out and puts his arm around her for comfort. "A man's got to do what needs doing . . . even when it scares the hell out'a 'em."

They both stand watching until the wagon rolls out of sight. With a sigh, Mrs. Cochran heaves her shoulders. "Well Papa, you's got stuff that needs doing, so get to it."

Mr. Cochran looks down at his tough, aged frontier woman and squeezes her to his side. She looks up at him and rolls her eyes before scooting away. He gives her a playful pat on the rump before she makes it up on the porch and through the door.

"Ohh, you rascal . . ."

The dust begins to settle around the wagon circle. All the attacking riders have pulled back, and only the occasional shot rings out from the surrounding scrub brush and rocks.

Behind the wagons, everyone stands ready for the next onslaught. The injured are laid out at the center of camp near the cook fire where they are cleaned and bandaged. Several women crouch low or crawl on their knees, tending to their tasks.

Bouncing and rocking along through the desert terrain, Holton ducks away as Bear nearly brushes the wagon against a large cholla cactus tree. He gives Bear a reprimanding look, then suddenly perks his ears into the distance. Holton listens intently as he tries to hear past the sound of their creaking wagon. He squints and cocks an ear to the breeze, then pats Bear's arm. "Hold back and save the team."

Relaxing the reins, Bear eases the team into a walk. "What's cookin'?"

Listening again into the wind, Holton stands in the box and looks out ahead.

"We're getting close, and there're no sounds of a fight."

"Suppose we're too late?"

"Too quiet for looting."

Disengaging himself from the supplies and gear in back, Ryan scoots forward and peers out. Holton sits back down, and Ryan puts his hand to his shoulder. "Why are we slowing down?"

Holton glances back at him. "We need to wait for the next attack."

"What?"

"To have 'em out in the open and fighting will give us the most effect."

"What if they don't attack?"

"They will."

Visibly flustered, Ryan clings over their shoulders. "We need to get in there as soon as we can!"

Bear slaps the reins and the team gives a jump, sending Ryan tumbling back into the wagon. "Sit down, kid! You do as Holton here says and you may live through this yet."

Thumbing the hammer on his rifle, Holton sits ready. He glances back at Ryan. "Keep your rifle handy and get prepared for a fight, kid."

Ryan settles down into the wagon bed and gets low behind a saddle with his rifle ready. Holton glances over at Bear. "You ready for this, Bear?"

"Ready 'nd rarin' . . ."

Chapter 21

Assembling at the top of the rise, the Indians look down on the wagon circle. Even in silhouette, the flare of their horses' nostrils and the pumping of nervous muscles radiate energy. With a blood curdling war whoop, the hilltop seems to explode in movement as the horseback natives descend on the wagon train in a renewed assault.

The horses thunder down the embankment, greeted by heavy fire from the wagon circle. After the first barrage, Indian foot soldiers pop up from the nearby brush and charge the wagons' perimeter.

The supply wagon driven by Bear and Holton crests the hill and looks down on the continued attack at the wagon train circle. Putting his rifle easy to his shoulder, Holton pulls back the hammer and looks at Ryan in the wagon. "Here we go, kid . . ."

He watches as Ryan readies his gun and hunkers down in the crates and burlap bags of supplies. Holton turns to Bear and nods. "Let's get to it."

Teeth gritting, Bear stands in the wagon box, gives the reins a slap and hollers. "Like I said . . . I was born rooster'd 'nd rarin' to go!"

All at once, the horses flex under the touch of the reins and dig in. The horse team breaks into a run, and the wagon charges down the hill at the attacking Indians circling the wagon train.

Bear tirelessly slaps the leather reins, and Holton and Ryan hold on to keep from being thrown from the charging wagon as it hops and skips down the rocky embankment. The wagon hits the bottom of the valley and charges toward the melee. Holton shoulders his rifle and snaps off a few shots. "Run 'em down, Bear, head-on!"

"You bet!" Bear turns the wagon with a spray of sand and rocks and drives it straight into the oncoming horseback Indians. Levering his rifle, Holton drops several warriors from their horses. As the Indians rush past, Ryan shoots from the rear of the wagon.

The wagon train defenders watch in renewed hope as Bear drives the supply wagon several passes around the wagon circle. The Indians' attack becomes a mass of confused riders as they dodge and flee the charging supply wagon.

From horseback, the wagon master rides over, hollers out to several able-bodied men, and ushers them at one of the unhitched wagons.

"Pull one of them wagons aside and let 'em roll in."

One of the wagons is slowly pushed aside to make an opening for Bear and the supply wagon. Instantly, a horseback warrior rushes past the wagon master. With a vicious whoop, he rides in and puts an arrow into one of the women tending the wounded.

Quick to react, the wagon master's pistol barks, and the warrior drops from his horse into one of the nearby cook fires.

"Git him out of there! Make sure no more of them Injuns break through!"

Still charging the attacking horseback Indians, Bear stands and urges the team on. Suddenly, he catches an arrow in his chest and slumps forward, almost falling into the running horse team. Holton quickly grabs him and pulls him back to the seat. "Kid. Pull him back there with you!"

Tossing aside his rifle, Ryan scrambles to the front of the charging wagon and grabs Bear by the shirt. He pulls him to the back, and Holton grabs the reins and quickly regains control of the team.

With rifle in one hand and reins in the other, Holton shoots an oncoming Indian from his pony. He levers the rifle one-handed and tucks it across his lap as he steers the supply wagon toward the gap in the wagon circle.

The Indian attack is broken with confusion, and the warriors begin to disperse and retreat over the hill. Steering the supply wagon into the defensive circle, Holton pulls the team to a halt. He grabs hold of his Winchester and continues firing on the remaining attacking Indians.

Riding up, the wagon master peers over the side of the supply wagon. He winces as he looks on at Bear, who sits painfully tugging at the arrow stuck in his chest. "Hold still there, fella. We'll get someone to help you git that arrow out." The wagon master eases his horse up next to Holton in the wagon's driver box. "I didn't think you boys had made it."

Holton lowers his rifle as the last of the attacking hostiles ride away over the ridge.

"Some of us didn't."

Bear continues to wiggle and tug at the arrow, making everyone queasy. Holton looks from Bear up to the wagon master. "Anyone around who can get that arrow out of 'em?"

"Sure thing."

The wagon master waves a few men over, and they lift Bear from the wagon. Holton climbs down from the front of the wagon and helps. They move Bear to the ground, and he smiles painfully. "Boy, Holton, we make a fine wounded pair."

Giving Bear a pat on the shoulder, Holton lets the other men lift and carry him away. Holton smiles after his old friend. "You'll be good as you ever was in no time."

Bear winces as he gives the arrow another tug. "I guess that's all I can hope for. I'll ne'er play the fiddle again . . ."

The wagon master, still horseback, rides over and looks down at Holton questioningly.

"Did he play the fiddle before?"

Holton rolls his eyes as he watches Bear enjoying all the attention he's getting from the crowd. "Not that I ever heard."

They carry Bear over to an area where womenfolk continue tending the wounded. He howls in pain, and they cluster around him.

With rifle in hand, Jeff Ryan crawls out from the back of the supply wagon. He turns meekly to Holton. "I guess I owe you a lot of thanks."

"You made your own decisions."

"Well, you've got my gratitude."

Holton looks out over the many families in the wagon circle as they reunite in euphoric sentiment of survival after the conflict. "Go 'nd see to your family." Ryan nods and runs off.

Holton walks to the edge of the wagon fortifications and scans the dead Indians and wandering empty-backed war ponies. He watches a long while for any threat of another attack. Finally, he feels the adrenaline in his system wane from the fight.

Exhausted, he slides down next to a wagon wheel and looks toward the numerous wounded scattered around the center of the wagon circle.

He watches as Ryan embraces his family. Observing the young man with his wife and two children conjures a longing sorrow inside Holton that makes his heart ache.

His attention is turned to the sound of Bear hollering in a foul-mouthed profession of pain. A slight smile creeps across Holton's lips as he listens to them pull the arrow out among Bear's wailing cries. The afternoon sun bakes the sandy ground. The smell of smoke and hot blood stagnates in the warm air of the surrounding valley.

Chapter 22

The long line of wagons is assembled and ready to move out. Perpetually horseback, the wagon master rides up and down the line inspecting rigs and loads. He gives a saluting wave as he rides past the supply wagon with Holton and Bear.

Bear sits with the reins cradled in hand and a bandage around his middle. In the back of the wagon, Holton sits with his legs kicked up. He notices Bear make a grunt as he stretches his bandaged side. Holton cranes his neck and hollers to the front of the wagon. "You alright up there, Bear?"

"T'was jest a scratch."

"The way you screamed out and cried, I thought a woman was birthin' a child."

"Not hardly."

Loping his horse down the line of wagons, the wagon master whirls his hat in the air.

"Move 'em out! Wagons roll!"

Bear adjusts himself, slaps reins, and the wagon lurches forward. "That arrow hit a long ways from my heart."

Holton laughs and smiles as he looks out the back of the rig and watches the long train of wagons snake out behind them. Dust rises in their trail as the dry desert is churned through iron-framed wood-spoke wheels.

The wind snaps the American flag jauntily in the center of the fort as uniform-clad troops march around the parade grounds of Fort Davis. The clank of metal and the sound of horses make for a healthy-sounding military post.

Inside the Officer's Barracks, Lieutenant Colonel Merritt paces before several of his officers who are assembled in his office. He stops a moment, and with growing frustration, he turns to face them.

"This is outrageous! We have a band of three hundred Apache terrorizing our settlements, and we can't find hide nor hair of them out there in this wasteland." Merritt pounds his fist onto the map hanging from the wall. "We need to bring this Malfonte in before the situation becomes a national embarrassment."

Adjusting himself uncomfortably in the straight-back chair in front of Merritt's desk, Captain Parker covers a cough and waits for Merritt to turn around. Merritt finally turns and passes a steely gaze over his officers. Captain Parker clears his throat.

"Sir. They split into smaller bands and leave false trails. We don't have enough scouts to trail them efficiently. The bands that we can follow head north where there isn't enough water for man or horse."

Merritt puts his hands behind his back and stares down his officers. "How can they travel through?"

Captain Parker turns from Merritt's gaze and looks over to Sergeant Hawkins. Sitting straighter in his chair, Hawkins addresses the commanding officer. "The Apache travel very light and have no qualms about eating a horse or two."

Merritt glares at his two officers. "Our horses, I assume?"

Sergeant Hawkins nods silently. Merritt looks over the men gathered in the room an excruciatingly long moment then turns back to the wall map of West Texas.

"We need to take the battle west to Bravo. Cut them off from the north. We can't risk them attracting any more troublesome Apache lodges from the New Mexico territory."

Taking notes on a pad of paper, Captain Parker raises his pencil to gain Merritt's attention. "What about recruiting more Indian scouts?"

Merritt paces in front of the map a while then turns to face the room. "It takes an Apache to catch an Apache . . . These scouts we currently have, can they be trusted?"

"Most of them can be."

Merritt nods and thinks a moment. "What about that fellow Holton Lang? He knows the Indians and from the stories I hear has no loyalty to the Apache anymore."

Captain Parker pauses writing on his pad and looks up at Merritt. "He headed west with Bear Benton and that wagon train that passed through a few weeks ago. Correspondence has been directed to Arizona."

Nodding, Merritt looks across the room to a window that views the parade grounds.

"Bear, too? I thought it'd been quiet around here of late."

He looks back toward Captain Parker and leans forward on his desk. "Get a message out to bring him in for special services. Get Benton back here as well."

"Yes, Sir."

Standing tall, Merritt tugs the front of his uniform tunic to straighten it. With a stern and steely gaze that exemplifies his authority, he addresses his officers.

"We're going to break up the Apache stronghold. This will be one for the history books. We are going to bring Malfonte into custody or leave him on the battlefield. Understood?"

Alone and parted from the group, the supply wagon driven by Bear steers through a lush grass- and tree-filled valley very much different from the dry rocks and sands of southern Arizona. The breeze flutters Bear's neckerchief as he puts his nose to the wind and takes a deep, inhaling lungful.

"Ahh, you can nearly smell the tops of the pines."

Climbing over the bench from the back, Holton settles in next to Bear on the driver's box seat. "It is a nice change from Texas."

"Ol' Charlie Nichols' place is just over there, around the bend and below that butte."

Scanning the surrounding green-fringed mountains, Holton puts his foot up on the front of the box and relaxes, easy, in the cooler air of the higher elevation. "How do you know this feller?"

"Oh, we used to run around a bit Missouri way. That was well before the war. He taught me a lot about everything. We'd hunt and trap near anything with legs and a hide."

"Near anything?"

Bear gives Holton a sidelong glance and smirks. "Taught me how to skin skunks, too."

Holton nods with amusement. "There a big profit in that?"

"It's a niche market. They ain't half bad to smell when you get that scent gland out of there. Had us a baby one once that couldn't squirt, and he was as tame as a kitty."

"Wonder how you got the name Bear after wranglin' skunks for a time?"

"Bear came later."

Smiling, Holton takes a deep breath and eats up the landscape with his gaze. The wagon creaks along peacefully as he studies the terrain. "I think I'd like to have a ranch out here someday."

"Well, do I have a surprise for you!" Giving the reins another slap, Bear urges the team on through the lush valley.

Chapter 23

The sun filters through dirty windows, illuminating the heavy dust hanging in the air. Merritt sits at his desk and fills out paperwork. His pen scratches away at the paper until there is a knock at the door. Looking up as the door cracks open, Merritt motions his personal aide into the room. The young man steps up to the desk and lays a pile of papers before Merritt. "Here are some orders that need your signature."

Putting his pen down, Merritt sits back in his chair and stretches his neck and flexes his shoulders. "Which ones?"

"The usual. And the special request for Benton and Lang."

Lifting them from the desk, Merritt scans several of them to find the one he is looking for. He signs one of the orders in particular and hands it back. "Get that one out as soon as possible."

"Yes, Sir."

The officer's aide snaps off a salute, spins on his heels, and marches through the door, closing it behind him.

Merritt turns to the window and looks out at the Cavalry troopers marching and drilling horseback. He stares a long while, lost in thought.

Finally, he wipes a reminiscent tear from his eye, smoothes the front of his uniform, and resumes his writing.

A ramshackle ranch entrance appears in the trail. The faded sign is weather-worn and barely hangs on by the rusty hardware holding it up. The large upright posts have a distinct lean as if they were going to give up the effort to stand at any time. Holton looks to Bear as they pass through the crooked gate. Looking around, Holton eyes the overgrown fence row. "Could use some upkeep."

"Ol' Charlie never was big on makin' things pretty."

The supply wagon rolls up the lane and rattles to a stop in front of a good-sized log ranch house with a broad front porch. Several dogs run at the wagon, circling it and barking. Bear follows Holton's gaze as they study the disrepair and unkempt buildings and fences. They climb down into the swarming dogs, and Holton peers over the wagon team at Bear. "He still live here?"

"Hope he's alright . . . could be dead by now."

Holton looks around at the ranch's appearance of abandonment. "From the looks of it, he may have been gone a while."

Bear scoots a yapping dog from his path.

"Who feeds the dogs?"

"Dogs don't need much."

The two approach the wide porch, and the front door swings open with a dragging creak. The distinctive clunk of a side-by-side double-barreled shotgun breaking closed and the click of the hammers pulling back stop Bear and Holton in their tracks. They peer into the dark shadows on the porch as the scuffle of feet comes through the doorway.

"Who's there! Speak up now or I'll let loose."

Taking a few steps away to the side, Holton gives Bear a sidelong glance. With a slight embarrassed cough, Bear calls out. "Hey now, Charlie. It's me, Bear."

"Who?"

"Yer old pal from Springfield, Missouri."

"Springfield? Tis a fer piece."

"Yes, Sir. Been travelin'."

"I don't know anyone out here from them parts."

"I was out ta visit a few years back."

"Lawrence?"

Bear shoots an awkward look at Holton, who has eased over to the shelter of some old empty barrels.

"Yeah, Charlie, it's me. Put that scattergun up."

Leaning toward them squinting, his eyes to near slits, Charlie lowers the shotgun and scans the area in front of him.

"Is there someone with you?"

"Yes, Sir. This here is Holton from Texas."

"Texas, huh? Well, he's either good folk or full of hot windys. They don't seem to have much between."

Bear laughs and Holton smiles in agreement. He steps from behind the empty rain barrel and gives a wave. "Pleased to meet you, Sir."

Easing the hammers down on the shotgun, Charlie relaxes and waves them up onto the porch.

"Come'n up here so I's can see ya."

The two walk up on the porch and look around at the general dishevel. The porch looks to be the catch-all for the house and ranch. The numerous dogs take up residence on random pieces of furniture, blankets, and old supply crates.

"Step some closer, Mister Holton, it's a mite dark here under the shade."

As Charlie leans in uncomfortably close and squints, Holton looks over questioningly to Bear. Charlie turns to Bear then slowly reaches up and touches his old friend's bearded chin.

"You run with the name Bear, huh? With them whiskers, it's no wonder. You're as furred up as a griz."

Turning back to Holton, Charlie scrunches and squeezes his face into a squint again.

"I know what you're thinking, fella."

"What is that, Sir?"

"You're thinking, this old codger caint see past the end of his nose nor if it's night or day." He turns and shuffles over to an old chair on the porch. Swatting a dog from the chair, Charlie rubs his eyes and sits down with a sigh.

"Well, you'd be right. Mine eyes are near all used up. Blind as a mole's ass. I might as well be straight up with ya since it's as obvious as a three-legged horse on a milk wagon."

Exchanging amused looks, Holton and Bear follow onto the porch and take up chairs. Bear swings his chair backward, straddles the seat, and faces Charlie. "You here by yourself?"

"I got my dogs and a few tame Indians that come around to help sometimes. Don't get many other visitors."

Adjusting in a wobbly chair, Holton braces himself as if it might break. He scans the clutter on the porch and looks to Charlie. "How do you keep up the place?"

Giving a chuckle, Charlie lays the shotgun across his lap and runs his fingers over it caressingly.

"Hell, you must be blind too? I imagine the place has nearly fallen down around my ears and looks like hell's backyard."

Adjusting himself in the creaky chair, Holton settles in to the best position to keep it from giving out. "Nothing that can't be fixed."

Charlie turns to Holton and looks serious a moment.

"Tell you what kid . . . You prove the place up some, you kin stay as long as you like. Eats ain't great 'round here, but the dogs don't complain much. Sure wishin' I lost my sense of taste 'nstead of my eyes."

A dog wanders up to Bear and begs for attention. Reaching down, Bear scratches the dog behind the ears, smiles, then sniffs his fingers. A queer look crosses his features as he gives them another sniff. He looks around and rubs his fingers on his britches before patting the foul-smelling dog away.

"If you ain't particular to eating like an Injun, Holton can fix things up right tasty. Hell, he's cooked stuff you'd n'er imagine to eat."

Charlie relaxes his squinting eyes, and a smile moves across his wrinkled features. "Well, that sounds jest fine."

Slapping his hands together, Holton rubs them in an exaggerated motion.

"I'll start right now! Are there any of these dogs you ain't particularly attached to or kin live without?"

The smile drops from Charlie's face as he bolts up in his chair, the shotgun nearly falling to the ground. The dogs turn and look up at him from their positions at his feet as he gasps in horror. "What!"

Bear roars with laughter as Holton leans back in the rickety chair and waits for the joke to settle in on Charlie.

Two of the dogs slink off, and Charlie leans down and pats the remaining ones at his feet. He looks up at Holton and shakes his head only slightly amused. "You part Injun or something?"

"Jest my stomach."

"Well, let's keep my barking pals out of the cook pot. I'd ruther be hungry than lonesome."

"Fair 'nough."

Charlie squints over at Bear, who continues to bellow with laughter. "You think that's funny, do ya skunk lover!"

Bear falls backward off his chair onto the porch and just lies there convulsed in thunderous amusement. "Ol' Charlie, how I missed you!"

Charlie looks to Holton and hooks a thumb over toward Bear. "Touched is he? He ain't changed a bit."

Watching Bear gasp for breath between laughs, Holton shakes his head, amused. "No, Sir."

The sky is clear, and a gentle breeze sweeps through the low-hanging trees. Holton fixes some corral fencing with several of the dogs sunning themselves nearby. He hammers a rail in place and wipes the trail of sweat that runs down from his hat.

A low growl wakes some of the dogs from their slumber, and, in unison, they all begin to rumble. Holton looks up from his work to see an old Indian figure walking down the lane. The old man gives a polite wave, walks over to a willow tree, and cuts a switch. A few of the dogs yelp and run off as the Indian waves the switch through the air. He continues down the lane to the cabin and goes around back.

Sitting in the shade of an oak, Charlie eases himself to his feet and shuffles over to the corral where Holton works. He leans on the top rail as a pup growls and yelps from behind the cabin. Holton drops the hammer in a wooden bucket and looks questioningly to Charlie.

"What's going on?"

"He's training that dog to smell Injuns."

"The puppy?"

"Yep, that's the way it's done."

Holton winces slightly as the cries and whine of the dog continue. "All these dogs done that way?"

Picking at his teeth, Charlie spits over his shoulder. "Naw, most of them are strays that come here when they were grown. They just don't like that ol' Indian, Broken Tooth.

"I kin imagine why."

The sound of the puppy subsides, and Holton looks over to see Broken Tooth walk out from behind the cabin, give a wave, and continue down the lane. Charlie watches Holton's gaze and scratches the stubble on his cheek.

"With my health and eyes, I need a good Indian sniffer to warn me. Most tribes 'round here are pretty friendly, but as more immigrant folks come in, the natives are getting pushed awful hard and getting ready to push back."

Holton looks to Charlie and nods. "It's that way all over."

"Most likely keep gettin' worse until someone wins."

Looking off to the horizon, a pained look crosses Holton's features as he thinks of Miryan. "No one wins; there will only be losers."

"Spect so." Charlie rubs his milky eyes, and Holton wanders away and sits on a nearby rock. Removing his hat, Holton puts it on his lap and rubs it with his thumb and forefinger. He looks up to the mountains, and a mist glazes over his eyes. The memories of his lost love still weigh heavy and tear at his chest. He takes a deep breath and sighs as the moisture wells up in his eyes.

Looking at his hard worn hands, he thinks of children and their tiny fingers. A tear runs down his cheek, and he flashes to wiping away tears of happiness from his lover's cheek. The sun flashes through the swaying branch of a nearby oak, and the image of Miryan kissed by the sunlight pulls at his aching heart.

A rare feeling of deep loneliness sweeps over him as he puts his elbows to his knees and stares at the ground. His dark mood is broken as he looks over to see Charlie still standing by the fence. Charlie wipes his eyes again and shuffles away toward the cabin. Holton's own aloneness seems to pale in the sight of the old man and the ranch. In that moment, a familial bond forms between the two men who have had to mourn the joys of life.

Chapter 24

Rifle shots and the screams of savage warriors fill the air as a small band of Apaches attack a log plank cabin. Rifles poke from the gun-port shutters and bark smoke and fire at the occasional brief target. Racing past, Apaches drop from their ponies and take cover behind ranch buildings and brush.

Two Apache braves ride horseback from behind the cabin with torches of smoking embers. Smoke begins to rise from the cabin walls followed by the lick of flames. Fanned by the dry West Texas wind, the crackle of fire roars, and soon the cabin is engulfed in a scorching inferno.

A family including Mama and child dashes from the blazing cabin and is quickly cut down by the Apache raiders. Screams of pain and war whoops from the Apache braves echo with the crackle of fire as the bodies are mutilated and ravaged. Trophies in hand and the cabin a fiery ruin, the Apaches ride from the gruesome site, leaving the unrecognizable bodies of the homesteading pioneers behind.

The Nichols' ranch is looking much improved as the weeks pass on. The spread is starting to look like a working operation again. Fences are mended and roofs are patched. Holton enjoys the work, which keeps his mind active and clear from painful musings. While Holton occupies himself with hard labor, Bear prefers to sit on the sidelines with a relaxing sense of watchful supervision.

The workday at an end, Holton cleans himself in the wash basin alongside the cabin. Throwing on a fresh shirt, he steps up on the porch where Charlie and Bear are just sitting down to the evening meal. Charlie folds his hands on the table and mumbles a prayer then looks to Holton as he sits.

"I sure do appreciate what you boys have done for me 'round here. I imagine the place ain't looked better."

Reaching out and filling his plate with food, Holton smiles toward Charlie. "It's a beautiful spread."

"Damn my eyes. I miss seeing that view the most."

Taking a mouthful of food then leaning back in his chair, Bear looks out at the valley and mountains. "When you set back awhile, you kin smell 'er on the breeze. That's one hell of a scenery."

Holton finishes serving himself a plate and glances up at Bear. "I oftentimes see you doing a lot of that settin' back, but all I can smell is you."

Mildly offended, Bear takes a sniff of his shirt and shrugs. He looks at Charlie and waves over to Holton. "I don't know why I put up with this feller."

He lets his chair down, shoots an amused look toward Holton, and continues to eat. Charlie laughs and sits quietly a moment while the others eat. The old man clears his throat and looks up at Bear and Holton "Either of yous ever put the thought to staying on here?"

Without lowering his fork, Bear chews and shakes his head. "Not me, I'm no rancher."

Holton grins through a mouthful of food. "I can vouch for that."

Bear looks up at Holton and grunts while Charlie puts his elbows to the table and turns to him as well. "How 'bout you, Mister Lang? This ranchin' life seems to suit ya well."

Holton puts down his fork and slowly looks from Bear to Charlie. He finishes his mouthful of food and shakes his head in agreement. "Yes, Sir. It do."

Charlie smiles.

"You interested?"

"I believe I would like to stay on a while."

Wide eyed, Bear continues chewing and lets his hands fall to the table. He shakes his head and laughs. "Golly, Holton. Most jest figure you for another military dispatch tramp. They'd a never known how you got roots just itchin' to grab hold someplace."

Charlie smiles and stirs the food on his plate. "Land is something to hold on to. A hard day's work on the land will heal a man of many a wound."

Bear shakes his head and scrapes the remainder of the food on his plate together. "Well, unless you plan on building a saloon over yonder, I'll probably not stay on for the duration."

Through years of hard-won wrinkles and whiskers, Charlie beams with the pride of a father. "Holton, if you don't mind bunkin' with an old blind codger, the place is yours when I pass."

The two watch surprised as Charlie pulls a yellowed piece of paper from his vest with some scribbles on it. "Here is the deed to the property."

Setting uneasy in his chair, Holton glances down at the property deed and shakes his head. "Now Charlie, this place should go to kinfolk."

"I don't have anyone else to leave it to, and you've earned it more'n anyone I know. I'd be honored to pass it on to you like you was family."

Holton looks to Bear, who only shrugs, stupefied. He takes a moment to think, then reaches out and covers Charlie's old gnarled hand with his. Charlie looks at him with his half-milky eyes, and Holton nods graciously. "I'm honored at your generosity."

"Then you accept."

"Yes, Sir. I'll continue on at the place."

"Good." Charlie reaches over and takes Holton's hand in both of his and gives it a shake. He pats the top of their clutched hands and nods toward the property deed. Holton sits back while Charlie rises and grabs up a pen and ink from a table near the door.

"Lawrence here . . . uh, I mean Bear, can be witness."

Leaning in close to the paper, Charlie makes his mark at the bottom. He passes the paper to Bear, who looks it over then signs it. With a knowing smile, Bear then passes the paper to Holton.

Looking at the men around the table, Holton finally looks down at the deed to the ranch property. Bear smiles as he watches Holton sit uncomfortably for a long moment, then signs.

"Well, Holton, you ol' homesteader . . . it looks like you got roots again."

Charlie stands and extends his hand. "We'll shake on it again."

Standing, Holton takes hold of Charlie's hand and shakes. For a moment, the two exchange a mutual look of paternal love and respect.

"Thank you, Son."

"Thank you, Sir."

Bear claps his hands together and roars.

"This calls for a celebration! I do believe there is a jug in the wagon just for this occasion."

The evening has set in and the sounds of night emerge loud and clear from the surrounding darkness. Holton and Bear sit on the cabin porch steps with a jug between them. In the rising moonlight, they look out at the mountains and stars before them. On a padded bench behind them, Charlie quietly snores. His heavy breathing is almost comical as several dogs surround his feet and snore in similar manner.

Bear takes a snort from the jug and looks back at Charlie. "He's a good sort."

Holton nods and takes off his hat. He rubs the soft beaver felt brim between his fingers and works his way around the hat. "I don't quite know what to think about this."

Bear takes another swig from the jug and shivers. "He likes ya 'nd knows you'll take good care of this place 'til he's gone."

Running his fingers over the dirt-crusted cavalry cords on his hat, Holton thinks on where he is and who he's been. "He hardly even knows who I am."

"Hell, Holton. You ain't hard to figure. You tell it straight, and you don't mind a hard day's work. What else is there to know?"

"This ranch is worth something."

Bear takes another pull from the jug and wipes the dribbles from his chin whiskers.

"So is taking care of an old fella who knows his days are numbered and doesn't want all he's got to go to waste."

Holton nods and ponders his blessings in a different light. He gives the hat brim one last brush and places the worn cavalry hat back on his head. "It's a responsibility."

Bear nods his head and gives the jug a swish. "Yes, Sir."

He hands the jug over to Holton, who swings it around and tips it over his shoulder for a swig. Feeling the burn of its contents, Holton takes a deep breath and lets it out slowly. He looks over at Bear and passes the jug back to him. "You ain't up for sticking?"

"Maybe awhile. N'er gave it much thought before."

The young pup in "Injun training" walks over and gives Bear's boots a sniff. He looks up at him, then walks over to Holton and curls up near his feet at the bottom of the stairs. He momentarily looks up at Holton, then out to the mountains as well.

Bear reaches down next to the steps and grabs a leather rifle scabbard. He hands it over to Holton. "Found this in the wagon when I was huntin' the jug."

Taking the rifle scabbard, Holton turns it over and studies the rich leather.

Bear gives the jug a few more swishes, takes a gulp, gasps with the burn of corn liquor, and nods to the scabbard. "Went along with that winnin' rifle of yours. That little feller from the East was mighty disappointed that he didn't get to do a photograph with you."

"Thanks."

"I guess it's your day for gifts."

"Seems that way."

Bear takes another pull at the jug and sets it aside with a cough. "You are one lucky feller. Always hurts my pocket money to bet 'gainst ya."

Bear gives Holton a playful punch in the arm. They both startle as the Indian sniffing puppy jumps to his feet with a growl. Bear eases back when the pup leans forward and bares his teeth. A low, rumbling growl rolls out as the pup's eyes lock on Bear.

Holton looks from Bear down to the pup and leans forward, putting his hand out slowly.

"Easy, Dog."

The dog breaks its gaze from Bear and looks to Holton. The growl turns to a friendly pant, and Dog lies down with a watchful eye. Bear settles back on to the steps and shakes his head. "I'll be damned. That there pup has sure taken to ya."

"Yeah . . ."

"I guess he cain't smell your Injun part."

Holton nods as he looks the dog over. "I ain't much for dogs."

"Except when you're hungry."

Holton smiles, and Dog lets out a slight whimper. "You bet."

The pale purple of morning eases into the valley. Holton sleeps on the cabin porch floor with Dog curled up nearby. The puppy opens his eyes a moment, creeps toward Holton's feet a few inches, and goes back to sleep.

Over near the porch steps, Bear lies next to the empty whiskey jug. His eyes open a slit as he tastes his dried lips and parched mouth groggily. Sitting up slowly, he holds his head and winces. He looks around the porch, rubbing his face and the sleep from his eyes.

Yonder in front of the cabin, a few dozen yards away, a large deer buck walks slowly along. Bear watches as it raises its head, stops to look around, then begins to graze.

"I'll be . . ."

Putting his hat over his mussed hair, Bear slowly gets to his feet and holds his head painfully. In stocking feet, he creeps across the porch to his rifle near the door. As he steps near Holton, Dog lifts his head and bares his teeth, silently smiling a snarling warning. Bear tips his hat, smiles back, and grabs his rifle.

Moving quietly across the porch, Bear stops at the top of the steps and takes aim. Off hand, he slowly cocks the hammer. Lifting its head, the large buck turns to look at the cabin.

The explosion of the rifle shot reverberates and rattles the cabin's covered porch. Before the fresh meat hits the ground, Holton and Charlie are on their feet with weapons in hand. Dog is at attention and baring his teeth at Bear, while Charlie is whirling his shotgun around blindly.

"What the hell's going on!?" screams Charlie.

Dropping his rifle, Bear hollers and holds his throbbing head. Holton takes position at the porch railing and scans his rifle across the terrain. He yells over toward Bear. "Are you shot?"

Charlie jumps around with his shotgun looking every which way. "Who the hell is shooting?"

Holding his pounding head, Bear wails and sits on the steps. "Oohhhh! My head."

Spotting the rack of the buck, Holton lowers his rifle and slowly rises from his kneeling position. "That your shot out there, Bear?"

"Yeah, but I think I might have killed me head for it." Wincing, Bear looks out at the large rack lying still in the grass.

Charlie comes up behind them with his shotgun at the ready and squints frustrated. "What the *hell* is going on!!"

Holton and Bear turn to Charlie as he continues to look blindly in all directions. Holton puts his arm around Charlie's shoulder and pushes the shotgun barrel away as he speaks.

"Lawrence here just shot us some dinner."

Still cradling the throbbing in his head, Bear looks sternly over at Holton. "Easy there with the name callin', friend."

"Alright, Bear. Nice shot."

"Yeah, 'nd it jest took one."

Charlie sets down his shotgun and grabs up his knife from the table. "Fresh meat? Well, let's get to it and not wait for the coyotes to get at 'er."

Chapter 25

The familiar clang of military equipment on horseback comes from up the lane. A single US Cavalry soldier rides onto the ranch and approaches the cabin. Several dogs circle him with sniffs of inspection. Seeing the cabin empty, the Cavalry trooper steers his horse to where the fresh deer meat hangs from a large tree branch. Bear observes the rider as Holton and Charlie stand working nearby.

Bear wipes blood from his hands and motions with his knife. "Eh, Charlie, you expecting company?"

"Who is it?"

Holton stops work as a range of painful emotions swell inside him. "US Cavalry."

Putting his ear to the wind, Charlie winces. "The whole thing?"

Turning back to the work at hand, Holton speaks low to Charlie. "Nope, jest one rider."

Bear squints into the distance and studies the soldier. "I'll be, I think that's Fellows."

Leaning back against the corral a moment, Holton looks sick to his stomach. "From Texas?"

"Yeah . . ."

The soldier rides up and stops his horse before them. "Excuse me, gentlemen. I'm trying to find . . ." He looks down and identifies Bear. "Oh, hello, Bear. You're half the pair I was looking for."

"Hey there, Fellows. What's the other half?"

Fellows looks over at Holton but doesn't recognize him in his ranch clothes. Charlie watches Fellows glance toward Holton. The old rancher looks up at the Cavalryman and steps forward to address him.

"What's this about?"

Chewing his bottom lip, ruffling his chin whiskers, Bear nods as he sheathes his knife and wipes his hands clean. "Yeah, Fellows, what brings you way out west?"

Reaching into his saddlebag, Fellows pulls out an envelope. "May I step down?"

"Please do."

Fellows swings down from the saddle and hands the dispatch envelope to Bear. Holton hangs back on the corral rail wiping his own hands while Bear opens and reads the dispatch message.

Bear mumbles to himself for a bit as he slowly reads the military document. Finishing the read, Bear lowers the letter and looks up at Fellows. "How bad is it back there?"

"Half the Native scouts have quit and joined up with Malfonte. The others can hardly be trusted. I need to find Holton Lang as well. Do you know where he might be?"

Bear walks the letter over to Holton and hands it to him. "Here ya go, Holton."

A surprised Fellows quickly recognizes Holton and watches him read the letter quietly. Fellows gathers himself, straightens his uniform, and clears his throat. "Between Malfonte and Stalking Wolf, there are two large bodies of Mescalero Apache who have been raiding and killing every homesteader in the West Texas territory."

At the mention of Stalking Wolf, Holton looks up suddenly, and the parchment in his hand trembles slightly. "What of Stalking Wolf?"

"He is leading a second contingent of Mescaleros. They split off from the main body trying to separate our forces. They attack different locations simultaneously or come around lethally on the flank."

With the hairs rising on his neck and sensing the sudden tension, Bear turns to Holton questioningly. "You know this Stalking Wolf?"

"Yep."

Fellows watches as Holton steadies his hand and finishes reading the dispatch. "Time is of the utmost importance. I'll rest my horse for the night, and we'll leave at first light."

Bear takes hold of the bridle on Fellows' mount. "I'll be ready."

Watching Bear with the Cavalry horse in tow, Charlie sits on a stump and looks blankly into the distance. Holton glances over at him and folds the letter carefully. "I'm not going."

"But Sir, your presence is highly requested."

Holton shakes his head mournfully. "I was once a soldier, not anymore."

Bear takes a deep breath and looks quietly at the ground. Fellows stares with disbelief at Holton then looks to Bear without support. An awkward silence ensues until Holton offers up the dispatch, and Fellows steps over and takes the letter from his hand.

"Regardless, I have notified you of the situation and need to be returning on the morrow."

Holton nods and leans back on the corral. "You delivered the message."

Stepping up, Bear gives Fellows a pat on the shoulder. "C'mon, we'll take care of your mount. How's old Stone Britches at the fort?"

Bear leads Fellows and his mount to the barn. After they have gone, Charlie breaks from his stare and turns to Holton. "I understand if you have to go."

"That was another life."

"It was your life."

"It's dead to me now."

Charlie watches quietly as Holton walks away and Dog gets up and follows.

The early morning sun raises the dew from the ground and the haze of mist hangs in the chilled air. Holton stands near the corral and watches Bear as he packs and ties on his saddlebags. Bear looks to the dog at Holton's feet and gives a laugh. "That pup sure has a thing fer ya."

He rubs his horse's rump and scratches his cheek whiskers. "Our trail shouldn't be hard to find if'n ya change yer mind."

Holton nods and steps around toward Fellows as he mounts up. He puts his hand to the cavalry saddlebags, pats them down, and looks up at Fellows. "Hear of anything of the Mescalero lodge that once was Yellow Hawk?"

Turning his horse around, Fellows adjusts in his saddle and looks down at Holton.

"Not really, they're mostly scattered and trying to survive. A few have turned themselves in at the fort. The others are all considered hostile."

"Most of 'em ain't."

"With Malfonte and Stalking Wolf at large and swooping down on the settlements from who knows where, we cannot afford to make assumptions."

Stepping back, Holton clenches his jaw with that old sour military taste in his mouth. He looks past the two men on horseback out to the mountains and thinks of his once peaceful Apache home.

Fellows wheels around his horse and touches the brim of his hat in salute.

"We best be going. Good day, Mr. Lang. Thank you for your hospitality, Mr. Nichols."

Watching Fellows ride off down the lane, Bear lifts his eyebrows at Holton, understanding his inner conflict. He rides over alongside him and pushes his hat down on his bushy hair. "See ya, Holton."

Holton reaches up and gives Bear's leg a pat. "Yeah . . . see ya."

With a shrug, Bear looks down at Holton then nudges his horse into a lope off after Fellows.

Holton watches as the two riders travel east, side by side down the trail. He can see their horseback forms for almost a mile before they disappear over a rise. Dog looks back as Charlie quietly walks off and finds his chair on the cabin porch.

After a while, the faint trail of dust settles in the distance. Holton drops his eyes to the ground and walks to the woodpile. He grabs up the axe in his hand and, with solid deliberate swings, begins splitting wood.

Chapter 26

Inside the Officers' Barracks, Bear and Denny stand before Lieutenant Colonel Merritt at his desk. Merritt stands and paces back and forth before a topographical map of west Texas.

"This is where the Apache have been slinking off to after their attacks. We need to dig them out of those rocks." Exchanging worried glances, Bear and Denny look to each other then back to Merritt and the map. "From your looks and comments thus far, I can surmise that you don't want to follow the Apache into this hostile terrain."

Coughing into his hand and clearing his throat, Bear stands at attention before the Colonel. "Sir, followin' an Apache into them rocks would be like puttin' yer head into the mouth of a cougar to catch 'is tail."

Denny cracks a smile, and Merritt scolds him with a stern look. "Yes, I get the message Bear."

Leaning on his desk, Merritt takes a moment then looks up at the two scouts. "The question is this . . . how do we get the Apache out of those rocks so we can push them to the west? As you have stated, we cannot fight them on their own ground."

Glancing over at Bear, Denny takes a small step forward. "We may be able to use the Apache's own tricks to pull 'em out of there into the open."

Merritt nods and pounds his fist on the desk with increasing enthusiasm. "That is exactly what we need to do! I want Malfonte and his savages pulled from the Guadalupe Mountains and pushed west to Rio Bravo!"

Sitting under one of the larger shade trees, Charlie whittles at a piece of wood. He looks up to watch the pup follow Holton as he walks past with a box of tools. Charlie coughs to get Holton's attention. "Holton, come 'ere a moment,"

Setting down the box of tools, Holton walks over to Charlie with the dog trailing behind.

"Sit down a spell," Charlie ushers a seat. "I wanna talk with ya."

Holton squats down to his haunches, and the dog finds a spot in a patch of grass nearby.

"That dog sure has taken with ya."

"Yeah, seems to stick close."

"He's yours if ya want 'em."

"He does his own thing."

Charlie smiles and spits a stream of tobacco. He muses over his whittling project and thinks aloud. "Yeah, I guess he's what you'd call self-reliant."

"It's a fine way to be."

"Sometimes is."

Holton seems irritable and ill at ease. He looks around at the ranch, then over to the sun setting low in the sky. "What is on yer mind, Charlie? I've got some things to do before nightfall."

"Sit down."

Resisting for a bit, Holton finally sighs and relinquishes his work plans for the present. Easing to the ground, Holton sits and pushes back his hat. Charlie watches and studies him a long while and clears his throat.

"You got things to do, but they ain't 'round here. My eyes are nearly gone, but I ain't entirely blind. It aches my heart to say it, but you've got unfinished business that needs doin' back there with them Mescaleros."

Holton traces his finger in the dirt. He looks up at Charlie with pain glistening in his eyes.

"There is nothing there for me anymore."

"I don't know what you had or left back there, but it is still a big part of you."

"It's finished for me."

"The hell it is!" Tossing aside his whittling, Charlie wags his knife at Holton. "Tell'n ya the plain of it, you ain't been much of a joy to have 'round here for the past few weeks. Sure, lots of work gets done, but a man who's avoiding himself and hiding from his thoughts ain't much."

Charlie shakes his head sadly and tosses his knife down, sticking it in the dirt. "Living the truth is the makings of a man . . . 'nd you've been lying to yerself. That's no way t' keep on."

"I made a commitment."

"To this here ranch?"

"And you. I take the responsibility serious."

"Them stock have brands on 'em and are jest gonna do their own natural thing. The land will always be here. It's yours now and it'll wait." Charlie and Holton exchange a glance then both look away, almost embarrassed at their fondness for each other.

Charlie pulls his knife from the ground and wipes clean the blade. He muses to himself as he tests the sharpness of the blade's edge. Looking up at Holton, he smiles warmly upon him.

"As for me, I ain't long for this life. I've had a good run, and I thank ya for being a friend. My dying request would be for you to finish what business you have vexin' at you so's you can be at peace."

Charlie carefully slides the knife into the sheath on his belt without a blink or glance down. Holton turns away and stares out at the landscape. He puts his hands to his face and rubs his temples, trying to control his emotions. Finally, he faces Charlie, no longer trying to hide his sadness. His eyes show the pain from memories of lost love. "I don't know if going back there and finishing it will ever make it right for me."

Nodding with compassion, Charlie pulls a pipe from his vest pocket and loads it. "Ya do know it ain't working out for you being here." He lights the pipe and gives it a puff. "You feel inside what needs to be done. A man ought to do what he thinks is right, or he'll be running from his true self."

Holton glances back at Charlie and lets out a hint of a smile. "You're a good friend, Charlie."

Charlie continues on his pipe as they both sit in silence looking out at the terrain and setting sun. The puffs of cloud in the sky begin to show with color as the sun dips into the horizon.

The following morning, the weather is cold and damp. Holton comes in from early chores onto the porch followed by the dog. His shoulders are wet as he looks out toward the drizzle hanging in the air like a haze. Dog shakes himself and looks up at Holton, who steps inside the cabin. "Charlie, if you gonna sleep the day through, it's a good day fer it."

Dog walks quietly over to Charlie's bunk and gives it a sniff. As Holton pulls back the burlap cover from the window to let some of the dim light in, the dog whimpers. "What is it, Dog?"

Walking to Charlie's bunk, Holton senses a calm emptiness. The lines around Charlie's eyes that once strained for sight are finally relaxed to a truer vision. Holton stares down at Charlie, peaceful in his eternal rest. Dog looks up at Holton then quietly walks outside.

"Goodbye, my friend." Holton pulls up the blanket over Charlie's relaxed features and sits quietly in a nearby chair. The hazy drizzle outside turns to an easy rain that patters on the cabin roof. Holton sits and stares out the open front door with the dog curled up at the threshold. As the day passes, the rain falls intermittently, and Holton continues to sit and quietly stare out into the void.

Chapter 27

Fort Davis is alive with the sounds of marching Cavalry troops. Swirls of dust from the horse's hooves and rallying bugle calls fill the air. In a seemingly endless procession, mounted Cavalry troops ride through the front gates of the fort. Crowds of people, homesteaders and civilians, stand near the dusty road observing the company of troopers file past. As no activity at the military fort goes unnoticed, native sentinels on the nearby hilltops and mountains take to horse.

Moving east, the morning sun in his face, Holton rides along at a steady gait. Sitting easy in the saddle, he mentally prepares himself for the long journey ahead. Trailing behind the hoof falls at a measured pace, the dog trots along ever vigilant and watchful. With leather saddlebags filled and a blanket bedroll tied on behind the cantle, Holton travels light across the harsh Western landscape. His mind travels beyond his gaze over the hills and valleys, through the desert and sky, back to Texas.

Maneuvering his way through the rocks, Holton rides cautiously, watching for sign. With nose to the wind, the dog follows along a short distance behind. They ride quietly through the rocks with the unshod hooves of Holton's mount making only a muted tap on the ground.

The hot afternoon sun heats the sparse vegetation, which emits a thick, dry smell that fills the nostrils and hangs heavy in the air. Dog gives off a deep, rumbling growl, and Holton quickly ducks low and steers his horse to a squat, brushy scrub tree. He eases the horse backside into the cover of the tree branches and leans over to quiet the muzzle. The dog continues to grumble, and Holton shoots him a scolding look. "Easy, Dog, shh . . ."

Swallowing his growl, the dog looks up at Holton obediently. With a wag of his tail, he eyes Holton then slips out of view behind some nearby rocks.

Approaching on the ridge, four Apache braves ride through the brushwood talking quietly. Their conversation is muted and doesn't travel past their own ears. They pass within twenty feet of Holton's concealment and pause.

One of the Apaches stops and straightens in the saddle then looks around. Holton watches as the Apache turns his horse and rides toward him slowly. Lying nearly flat across his horse's neck, Holton strokes the horse's muzzle to keep it from calling out. His other hand reaches down to his revolver at his side and takes a ready grip, thumb on the hammer.

The Apache takes a few steps closer and stops at the sounds of rattling rocks a few yards off. He peers into the distance and listens intently. The other braves call out the Apache word "coyote" to their fellow warrior and continue on. After a moment's hesitation, the Apache turns his mount and rides on after the others.

A stream of perspiration rolls out of Holton's buckskin sleeve as he gives the horse a pat and eases back into the seat of the saddle. He pushes his wet, sweat-soaked hair back on his head and adjusts his hat.

Waiting a while for the Apache riders to get some distance, Holton eases his horse from cover and moves to pick up their trail.

Holton swings from his mount and studies the multiple sets of Apache tracks. He looks to the position of the sun and gages their direction of travel. Stepping into the saddle again, he turns at the sound of the dog coming through the brush.

"Good dog. Let's see where they lead us." Easing his horse on, Holton follows the rocky trail to where the four Apache riders converge.

The four Apache braves ride over the crest of the mountain and descend down into the valley of Malfonte's camp. Enormous and vast with hundreds of dwellings, the camp is filled with herds of war ponies scattered around. The braves pick their way down through the rocks past the watchful sentinels and ride into a lively Apache war camp.

From a high vantage point, Holton dismounts and looks down at the Apache hideout. He squats down on his haunches as he looks around at the distinct landmarks and studies the terrain. Committing the area to memory, he scans it, picking out the potential Apache lookouts. Finally, he leads his horse to an area of concealment and loosens the cinch strap. Dog sits nearby and watches as Holton settles in to make a cold camp.

The first light of morning finds Holton sitting at his vantage point eating hard tack and drinking from his canteen. Dog lays nearby, soaking up the early morning sun's warmth and quietly watching. Scanning the Apache village, Holton puts a keen eye to every rock and crevice. An hour passes before he finally breaks from his study of the hostile surroundings. He finishes the last bite of food and looks to the sunrise for a brief moment of enjoyment.

Closing the flap of his saddlebag, Holton buckles two of the three leather straps and picks up his bedroll. He moves to his already saddled horse and lays his cavalry bags over the saddle behind the cantle, followed by the rolled blanket. He ties the rawhide saddle strings, and his eyes dart to the dog when he hears a low, rumbling growl. "What is it, Dog?" Smoothing his hand along the seat of the saddle, Holton looks up as he jerks his rifle from the leather-skirted scabbard.

In the rocks not far away, an Apache draws back his bow, ready to shoot. Holton puts his rifle to his shoulder and snaps off a shot. The Apache releases his arrow, and it whizzes past Holton and sticks in the rocky sand behind him. Levering the rifle, Holton shoots again, this time hitting his mark. The Apache leaps into the air with a bullet hit to the heart and falls from his perch into the craggy rocks below.

The Apache camp in the valley starts to buzz with alarmed movement. Holton glances over the rim to the alerted camp and races back to his mount. "Let's get out of here, Dog . . ."

With rifle in hand, Holton swings into the saddle. As he wheels his horse around, another arrow whizzes past. With reins loosely in hand, he reaches up and takes aim with the rifle. He fires a shot into the rocks at another Apache, and the warrior disappears from sight.

Scanning the area then levering the rifle one-handed, Holton spurs his horse forward. Weaving through the large boulder–strewn trails, Holton, with the dog following, race away from the valley of the Apache camp.

The Apache camp is a mass of excitement as braves gather their weapons and dash to their mounts. The women pull their children from the path of galloping horses. Walking into the midst of the gathered warriors, Malfonte turns to address Stalking Wolf in native Apache tongue.

"Who could have found this camp? No white eye has dared to come close."

With a knowing look, Stalking Wolf turns away and leaps onto his waiting mount. Malfonte looks up at him with an insanely intense fire in his eyes. "Bring him to me!"

Stalking Wolf gives a war whoop that pierces the hectic commotion of horse and riders. He raises his war lance, shakes it with another blood-thirsty scream, and charges off, followed by dozens of Apache braves galloping in a cloud of dust.

Chapter 28

Holton rides hard, weaving through the sandstone canyons and valleys. He occasionally glances over his shoulder at his back trail looking for dusty signs of Apache pursuit. Close on his heels, the dog runs along with head low and tail tucked.

Reining his horse in at the edge of a large rock formation, Holton looks out over the empty expanse ahead in the landscape. While he lets his horse blow wind, he studies the vulnerable terrain looking for the nearest concealment. With a wince, he sees the best way is to charge across through the barren, wide-open middle. "Aw, damn . . . " he mutters.

He looks down at the dog and watches him pant slightly while looking up at Holton obediently. "C'mon Dog, it's now or never."

Sinking his spurs, the horse bolts, and Holton starts off across the open, sparsely vegetated terrain.

The hot afternoon sun bakes the dry, shade-free desert as horse and rider venture out across the empty terrain. Pulling his hat down on his head, Holton rides at an easy lope with a small trail of dust rising from his horse's hoof path. The dog follows close behind with his own trail of dust rising from his tracks. The heat of the day leaves stained rings of white chalky salt on Holton's buckskin shirt as the perspiration evaporates almost immediately.

Easing his horse to a restful but brisk walk, Holton lets dog catch up and regain his breath. Alone out in the middle of nothingness, he fills his lungs with air and closes his eyes in a moment of calming peace. Listening to the emptiness around him, Holton looks over his shoulder to see a cloud of dust on the horizon and seemingly dozens of Apaches in pursuit. He looks down at Dog, and they exchange a knowing look.

With still a lot of ground to cover, Holton pushes his horse into a lope and takes the direction ahead to the nearest outcropping of rocks. They continue to move along at an even pace until Holton glances back again and makes out the individual figures of the large assemblage of Apache ponies and riders. He urges his horse to a gallop as the Apache burst into the open landscape and fan out in angry pursuit.

The thunder of horse and hoof across the hard-packed ground emanates from the desert floor. The mass grouping of Apache riders screams at the sight of the lone rider on the horizon. With war lance and rifle raised, they tear across the open ground slowly narrowing the gap. Like a sandstorm rolling across the desert, the Apache close in.

Ever watchful over his shoulder, Holton gages the distance to cross before being overtaken. He spurs his horse on and tries to coax the bottom of the horse's endurance. The Apaches continue to gain in pursuit as Holton's horse begins to falter. "Come on, steed, not far to go . . . "

Nostrils flared, the horse's breathing sounds like the engine of a locomotive as his body pumps the muscled frame and legs that seem to fly over the ground. With one last burst of speed, the horse finally begins to flag. Holton slaps his reins against hide and continues to press on with the dog following not far behind.

From a gap in the rocks ahead, another dozen Apaches pour from the earth. Holton veers his horse away toward another outcropping of boulders, desperately trying to make it to the protection of the hills. The lighter horseback Apaches quickly cut the distance between.

Drawing his pistol, Holton reaches back and fires off a few shots at the quickly approaching riders. Several Apaches drop from their mounts at full gallop as hot lead spins them from their ponies. Finally, clicking on an empty chamber, Holton holsters his pistol and peels his rifle from its scabbard.

In a race against death, the mass of Apache riders trail the lone rider across the open desert terrain. Puffs of dust from the hoof prints of Holton's mount are consumed and overrun by the cloud of pursuing Indian war ponies. Holton spin cocks the rifle to his side and reaches out behind him to fire. He lets go a shot, and one of the Apache warriors disappears from his horse and is consumed by the horseback rampage.

Holton's mount begins to cough and play out. Urging the horse on, Holton turns forward and levers his rifle again. Lagging and winded, the horse suddenly stumbles and drops his front shoulder. In a cartwheel of sand, dust, and animal, Holton is launched forward as his horse tumbles.

With rifle in hand, Holton rolls and hits the ground running. He looks back to his horse still on the ground and rams his hat down on his head. Dog darts ahead, and they both make a mad dash for the rocks.

Quickly, the Apache horsemen overtake Holton and rush past him. A blow from the broadside of a lance spins him to the ground. He looks to an Apache with his lance trained on Dog and hollers, "Run, Dog!! Get away from here!" Dog cuts under the attacking Apache pony's legs and quickly disappears into the nearby rocks.

Coming up on one knee, Holton fires his rifle. With each working of the lever, an Apache is jerked from his mount. The Apache whirl their horses and charge Holton with their lances. Levering the rifle with cool precision, Holton drops several of his attackers until his Winchester rifle clicks empty.

The Apaches charge, and Holton deflects their lances the best he can. A war club comes down hard on his skull, knocking his hat askew and spinning him in a daze. An Apache leaps from his horse, tumbling Holton to the ground, and several other Apaches are quickly upon him, punching and kicking.

The smell of dirt and the feel of sand in his mouth is the last thing he is conscious of as the ferocious horde of Apache warriors descend on him. Amidst the sounds of charging horses and screaming Apache war calls, all is quiet a moment before Holton is beat into unconsciousness and blacks out.

Chapter 29

The Apache warriors return from the manhunt and approach the village stronghold. Holton is pushed from his mount and pulled by a rope attached to the ties on his hands. With his bound hands out before him, he trips and is dragged through the center of camp. Beat up and battered, he hangs loose in the bindings as he is pulled along the rough ground. Women and children gather and hit his body with sticks and rocks as he is paraded past.

His hand raised high to halt the procession, Stalking Wolf slides from his pony and stands over Holton's prone body. Holton looks up at him through the settling dust. With the last ounce of saliva in his parched, dirt-caked mouth, he spits at Stalking Wolf's feet. Angered, Stalking Wolf kicks sand into Holton's face and motions for two braves to pull him to his feet.

Holton stands before the hostile Apache, blinking the sand and grit from his eyes. Stalking Wolf leans in close and breathes heavily through flared nostrils. With hot, rotting breath, he barks his native tongue. "Man of Miryan, you are half blood."

He draws his knife and motions across his own scarred face. "You give me this . . . now I will cut the white blood from you."

Looking at Stalking Wolf, Holton grits his teeth and tries to spit at him again. Stalking Wolf reaches out and slaps Holton hard across his beat-up and bloody face. Holton falls back, wincing in pain. He quickly collects himself, stands tall, and calls out in the Apache tongue.

"You dishonor me. I want to be killed by a brave warrior, not by Stalking Wolf, the killer of women, children, and old men!"

A curious crowd gathers to hear the white man speak in their own language. Stalking Wolf is taken aback by the insult. He looks around furiously as he feels his command of the crowd waiver. "Quiet your lying tongue. You are white eye and enemy to the Apache!"

Holton raises himself up and plays directly to the hostile audience in fluent Apache tongue. "You fight only for Stalking Wolf. Many Apache are dead because of you and your betrayal of Yellow Hawk Lodge. You are a coward and traitor to your people!"

Bystanders whisper and motion toward Stalking Wolf. With his relatively new standing in Malfonte's war council, he feels the insecurity of his position. He looks around at the questioning faces surrounding him and becomes more embittered and enraged.

Stalking Wolf raises his knife to Holton's neck and turns his head skyward with a death cry. He is about to slice into Holton's jugular when a booming voice calls out from the crowd and stops everyone in their tracks: "Halt your blade!"

All attention is turned to the looming figure of Malfonte as he steps through the crowd with a commanding presence. He stands before Stalking Wolf, the two hard warriors facing off. Their eyes momentarily engage in a struggle of power before Malfonte pushes him aside with superior authority. "This man who speaks the words of the people will not die today by your hand."

With keen, piercing eyes, Malfonte studies Holton for a long while. Impressed by the stature and universal respect for the Apache war chief,

Holton musters up the last of his energy to stand straight under the scrutiny. With dry, blood-caked lips, Holton barely speaks. "You are wise to push this cowardly warrior aside."

A hint of a smile glimmers in Malfonte's eyes as he watches Stalking Wolf nearly burst with anger. He steps around Holton and leans in to whisper near his ear. "You will welcome death when it comes."

Glancing over at Stalking Wolf still fuming, Malfonte speaks to the Apache braves flanking him. "Take this white man away and secure him." Malfonte directs his eyes at Stalking Wolf. "No harm will come to him until I command it."

Two Apache braves step up and take hold of Holton, who nearly collapses in their grip. Malfonte continues to circle Holton, then stops and steps in close. Malfonte's dark pupils pierce into Holton's pale blue eyes. "First you will tell us the plan of blue soldier and his fort. Then I may let you die."

The Apache village sits quiet as the sky darkens over the secreted canyon. The pony herd grazes as wisps of smoke come from cook fires in wickiups. There is a quiet peacefulness in the air that hides the tension of a coming battle.

Inside a large dwelling, firelight reflects off the shirtless body of Holton as he hangs by rawhide ties from the roof support rafters. Malfonte, Stalking Wolf, and several others sit near the fire and talk quietly.

Standing, Malfonte approaches Holton. He gives him a poke with a knife, enough to make Holton wince, but not enough to break the skin. Malfonte smiles cruelly. "You are strongwilled for a white man. You have the strength of mind and will like the Apache."

He circles Holton, occasionally poking him with the knife until he flinches or recoils in pain. "You will tell us or you will die."

Holton clenches his jaw and tries to swallow the pain. "I don't fear death."

"But yours will be the most painful of deaths."

A silence hangs heavy in the air as Holton stares ahead, waiting for the next jab of torture. Finally, with a wave to the others, Malfonte sheathes his knife and motions to the exit, and they follow him out.

Holton watches half-conscious as they file out. The last to leave, Stalking Wolf, stops before Holton. The Apache grabs him by the neck with one hand and squeezes with an iron grip. Glaring menacingly into Holton's eyes, he smiles. "Would you like to have me kill you now, half blood?"

Holton forces a swallow through Stalking Wolf's grip and stares coldly back at him.

"You do what you want to do."

Stalking Wolf pushes Holton away in disgust and steps out. Holton's hanging body swings gently back and forth until it finally suspends motionless. Holton retreats inside himself mentally as the fire slowly burns down.

Chapter 30

The clouded moon puts out little light to the darkness as horses and gear quietly clank. A mounted company of US Cavalry travels through the night. The steady parade of hooves clopping and dragging along the ground gives the procession an almost hypnotically peaceful feel. Heads droop on chests of bodies in the saddle as the call to sleep overcomes some of the soldiers. A sergeant rides along the column and gently nudges the drifting bodies awake. The parade of Cavalry continues on into the darkening night.

Inside the large Apache dwelling, the remaining embers of the fire reveal the still suspended body of Holton. Between the shadows, a lone figure can be felt entering. Silently, like a mountain cat, the stealthy figure circles Holton and observes his almost lifeless body hanging from the center pole.

Half conscious, Holton opens his eyes. His body tenses slightly as he senses the presence of someone's breath close behind him. Without attempting to look around or raise his head, Holton lets out his breath and relaxes. "Come to finish me?"

A knife flashes out and shimmers past Holton's face in the dull light. His eyes close in prayerful musing and Holton moans out his wife's name with his last breath.

"Miryan . . ."

In one quick stroke, the knife slices through the air and cuts the rope above Holton's tied hands. He drops to the floor in a heap and takes a moment to regain his wits. Slowly, Holton sits up and rubs his raw, bloody wrists as he unties his bindings. He looks up to an Apache brave who looks familiar but could be just another face from the crowd. Holton chokes down the blood in his throat and croaks very quietly in Apache, "Friend?"

"I am Running Bird, and I am no friend to you."

Holton lowers his eyes and musters all his strength to rise to his feet. Standing painfully before Running Bird, he holds out his hands, palms up. "Who do I owe thanks?"

Running Bird sheaths his knife and stares at Holton. He looks as if he will leave, then bends down to pick up something. Turning, he stands before Holton and offers over the white man's equipment of knife, rifle, and gun belt. He nods, and Holton returns the gesture with gratitude.

Holton picks his leather shirt from the pile and slides into it. He tucks the tails into his britches and takes his weapons from Running Bird. "Why do you help me?"

"I am friend to the family of Miryan. You were good man to her. She is dead, and the Apache is finished with you. Go now."

Taking up his weapons, Holton leans his rifle on the wall and buckles on his gun belt. He pulls his revolver and checks the cylinder. Seeing that it is still loaded, six cartridges around, he snaps the side gate closed and looks up at Running Bird grimly. "Someday," Holton murmurs quietly. "I will kill Stalking Wolf."

Holton slides his pistol back in the holster, and Running Bird hands him his old beat-up and well-used hat. Running Bird nods with consent. "That is not a bad thing."

As Holton brushes back his hair and pulls the cavalry hat down on his head, Running Bird quietly slips out the door into the darkness.

The Apache village is quiet and dark as only the stars cast shadows on the silent structures. Holton exits the dwelling and cautiously moves through the camp. He maneuvers to the perimeter of the encampment and sees an old unattended saddle near one of the wickiups. Moving past, he quietly scoops up the saddle, blanket, and bridle.

Holton gently slips through the makeshift fence into the sleeping pony herd. With saddle in hand, he quietly eases up on the slumbering horses and slides the saddle over one of them. The small horse wakes with a grunt of dissatisfaction, and Holton gradually soothes him quiet.

An Apache guard walks near the horses and peers into the herd. Unmoving, he stares for a long while until turning away, satisfied that all is well. Rising up from the herd, Holton slips his foot into the stirrup and swings his leg over the back of the Indian pony. Without making a sound, he slowly weaves through the sleeping horses. Passing through the gate of sorts, he lifts a rawhide skin filled with water from a timber peg and slowly rides out of the camp.

The early sun rises over the Guadalupe Mountains, showing the first light of a brilliant Texas sunrise. Holton rides through the rocks away from the Apache stronghold, occasionally looking over his shoulder at his back trail. Stopping his mount, he maneuvers his back to catch the few rays of sun and feels its growing warmth.

Holton sits low in the seat and takes the bladder of water from the pommel of the saddle. Pouring some water into his cupped hand, he takes a sip. He drips more into his hand and splashes the rawhide-smelling water across his blood-crusted face. Tying off the leather skin, he wipes the cool water bag across his face to remove some of the old blood.

With rifle laid casually across his lap, Holton rides on through the rocky, sparsely vegetated terrain. Cresting a rise, he spots a cloud of dust ahead in the morning shadows that could only be a large group of horses and riders. The distinct and distant muted din of military tack and saddle gives Holton pause. A puzzled look comes over him as he mumbles to himself aloud, "Could be lost? What are US Cavalry doing this far into Apache country marching at daybreak?"

Holton glances behind him in the direction of the Apache compound. After thinking a while, he spurs his horse on toward the source of the hazy dust cloud rising in the morning light.

A small company of US Cavalry rides through the rocky, mountainous terrain led by Captain Parker and Denny. Everyone peers around nervously at the many outcroppings of rock that could be concealing hundreds of Apache. Spurring his horse, Captain Parker rides up next to Denny and addresses him: "We should have full daylight in an hour."

The two walk their horses along silently a while until Denny finally takes his eyes off the new day's horizon. "How far into these rocks do you want to go? The further in we go, the less our chances of coming out again."

Denny pauses to glance around at the imminent surroundings, then back at the captain.

"Traveling at night was one thing. Riding into these rocks in daylight is another kind of crazy."

"Not much farther. We need to draw them out."

"I thought the plan was for us to trick the Apache, not for them to trap us."

Captain Parker turns to Denny. "We will continue on until we have made contact with the Apache and then draw them out."

Denny turns his attention to a small trail of dust in the distance. "Alert your men, Captain, this may be it."

Squinting to the far distance, Captain Parker sees the lone rider. "A single rider?"

"Sometimes that's all it takes."

Falling back, Captain Parker turns to his sergeant. "Tell the men to stand ready."

The order is passed through the ranks, and Captain Parker rides up next to Denny again and watches him study the approaching rider. "Any change in our situation?"

Staring intently, Denny watches the man on horseback. As the horse and rider near, Denny bites his cheek apprehensively. Captain Parker watches the single rider and sees Denny show a hint of recognition. "Can you identify the rider?"

"Yeah . . ."

The captain looks at Denny questioningly and continues to watch as the rider nears. He raises his hand to halt the troop. "Sergeant. Halt the procession. Stand ready." With rifles pulled from scabbards, the troop waits, patiently watching.

Horseback, riding at an easy lope, Holton approaches the company of US Cavalry and pulls up his mount in front of Denny and Captain Parker. A smile cracks across Denny's lips as he notices Holton's worked-over and battered state. "Hello, Lang," snorts Denny. "You look like you've been through hell."

"Near enough."

Captain Parker moves his horse forward and inspects Holton questioningly. "Holton Lang?"

Barely acknowledging Denny, Holton addresses the captain: "You need to turn these men around and move 'em out of here now."

Looking back at his troops then around at the empty landscape, Captain Parker eases his horse nearer to Holton. "Excuse me, but on what information do you base this dire opinion?"

Holton looks from Captain Parker to Denny then quickly counts the number of troopers.

"There are about two hundred Mescalero Apache gathered for war less than a day's ride north of here. They're coming this way now."

Captain Parker looks skeptical. "And how would you know this?"

"Just parted company with 'em during the night. Barely slipped out with my hide."

Holton looks over his shoulder to the north. "First light most likely put them right on my trail."

Eyeing Holton and his beat-up face, Denny grins. "What's left of your hide . . ."

Holton nods and observes Denny smirking at his condition with obvious amusement. With a chuckle, Denny looks down at Holton's prize big loop rifle sitting across his saddle pommel. "And ya made it out with that rifle, too?"

Holton shoots Denny a sidelong glance and turns to Captain Parker. "Captain, you don't have nearly enough men here to stop the flow of Apache that will be pouring out of those rocks in a few hours."

"I don't see any."

"When you do, it'll be too late."

Setting back in his McClellan, Captain Parker ponders a moment then looks to Denny.

"What is your advice on this matter?"

"If half that many is coming, it would be better to retreat to better ground. We have been traveling all night, and the men's wits may not be about them for more 'n a running fight."

Grinding his teeth, Captain Parker finally turns in the saddle and looks at his company of men. He looks back at Holton and nods. "Alright, which way do you recommend?"

Holton looks past the company of Cavalry at the open landscape scattered with rock outcroppings. He glances at Denny, then addresses Captain Parker. "Back the way you came would be fine. There's no need to cover your trail."

Captain Parker looks to Denny, who nods with silent approval. Whirling his horse around, the captain barks orders at the sergeant and gives the signal for the retreat.

Shortly, the company of military horse soldiers is headed along its back trail with Holton and Denny bringing up the rear. Denny rides next to Holton and gives a grunt. "Holton Lang . . . couldn't stay away from Texas."

"Nope."

"Two hundred Apache, huh?"

"Yep."

The two reluctantly acknowledge each other as brothers in arms and follow in the trailing dust of the US Cavalry.

Chapter 31

The morning light spreading through the mountains finds the whole Apache village a mass of movement. Braves covered in battle attire ride painted war ponies between the dwellings, raising dust, mixing with the frenzy. Several bands of horseback riders tear out of the village in pursuit of the lost captive. Leading one of the larger groups, Stalking Wolf lets out a blood-curdling whoop as he rides away.

Looming tall, with bloody knife in hand, Malfonte stands in front of the dwelling where Holton was held captive. He watches hundreds of braves whirl around him and prepare for battle. The energy in the camp seems to lift him and make him swell with malevolence.

In the doorway, Malfonte bends down to a bound Apache guard on the ground. With crazy, intense eyes, Malfonte stares at him with his throat cut and freshly bleeding out. He dips his finger in the warm blood and smears it across his forehead. With an amazing burst of energy, Malfonte springs from the ground and leaps horseback. He spins the mount and calls out to the Apache. "We will swoop down on them in their homes and cleanse the intruders from the lands of our people."

Screaming his war cry, Malfonte leads the hundreds of horseback Apache braves from the camp.

In command of the small company of US Cavalry, Captain Parker trots at the front of the column. The troopers ride anxiously but wearily from their long night ride. Trailing behind, just past the dust cloud, Holton and Denny bring up the rear.

Long-legged astride his horse, Denny scans the surrounding rocks and watches to the mountains behind them. "I didn't 'xpect to see you again. Bear said you settled down on some land in Arizona."

Holton glances over his shoulder again, scanning the terrain and rocks behind them.

"Yep, nice little ranch."

"What are you doing back here in Texas?"

"Unfinished business."

Denny glances over at Holton's wounds bleeding through his buckskin shirt. With a nod, Denny motions back toward the Apache rocks. "You get 'er finished back there?"

Holton turns to him and senses his understandable fear of being so far into hostile territory. He bears witness to Denny's apprehension of the Apache about to descend upon them. Holton shakes his head to the negative.

"Not yet."

The yap of a dog catches their attention, and Holton turns in the saddle to see Dog running full tilt out from the rocks. Denny watches the dog run toward them and looks at Holton questioningly. "You know that dog?"

"Yeah."

They hold up their horses a moment, waiting for the mangy puppy.

"He yours?"

"Nope."

"Where'd he come from?"

"He's been traveling with me some."

Holding his horse back and rearing into a spin, Denny looks to the Cavalry company riding ahead and waits for the dog to catch up. "What's his name?"

"Dog."

Denny looks strangely at Holton and rolls his eyes. The dog stops next to Holton's horse and looks yonder into the rocks. In the faraway distance, a hint of a churning cloud of dust begins to rise from many horses moving fast.

"Good eyes, Dog."

Slightly amazed, Denny watches as Holton nods to him, jabs his heels into his mount, and rides up to Captain Parker at the head of the column. The dog follows on his heels, and Denny rides after them.

Holton eases alongside Captain Parker and gestures over his shoulder. "Capt'n, if it's Apaches you want, you're about to have 'em in spades."

Captain Parker turns in the saddle and looks back at the ever-rising dust cloud forming.

"How soon until they're upon us?"

"Hour, maybe two."

"We need to lure them out of the mountains."

"Well, they're a'comin'. What then?"

Glancing over his shoulder, Captain Parker takes a deep breath and sits taller in the saddle.

"There are supposed to be reinforcement troopers placed who will drive them west to the Bravo River."

Denny rides up and addresses the captain. "We got a long ways to go 'fore we get clear of these rocks."

"Well, we will just have to keep on." Captain Parker waves a dismissive salute toward Holton and Denny and turns to his sergeant. "Double time, Sergeant!"

The Sergeant bellows orders, and the company of Cavalry picks up the pace. Exchanging concerned looks, Denny and Holton fall back and follow along. The clank and ground churning from the quick pace of the troopers makes a synchronized din as they cut through the sparse desert landscape.

Flowing through the imposing rock formations, hundreds of Apache surge over the passes and canyons. Like the head of a serpent, Malfonte leads the war party slithering horseback through the desert mountain rocks and terrain. The painted mass of men and horses makes for an awesome sight as they blur past the rock, leaving a cloud of sand and dust in their wake.

Chapter 32

Near a sparse outcropping of boulders, Stalking Wolf sits with a small band of warriors. They watch the procession of US Cavalry trot along through the valley below. Looking from the small company of blue coats to his eager band of Apache braves, an evil smile spreads across his features.

To the north, the increasing cloud of dust from the larger band of Apache takes the form of a conical twister. Stalking Wolf looks down to the column of Cavalry below. "We will wipe the blue coats from our land!"

With the prodding grunt of horses and choked-back war whoops, Stalking Wolf leads the band of warriors down through the rocks to the unsuspecting horse soldiers below.

Trailing behind the troopers, Holton rides next to Denny. He pretends not to notice Denny stealing glances at his bloody wounds and prize rifle. Holton edges his horse closer to Denny's. "How many troopers will intercept near the river?"

Denny turns to Holton and gives a skeptical shrug. "Dunno. Could be a company or could be the whole shebang."

The two bounce along at a fast trot, and Holton turns in the saddle to face Denny. They exchange a telling look of past military experience and understanding. "So . . . it could be jest us?"

"Yep."

"Sounds promising."

With a disheartened smile, Denny shrugs again and lopes his horse a bit to catch up with Holton. "That's the military for ya. We've been out eight days with no word from the fort or anyone else. We've been traveling at night for the past few shifts and have been in the saddle without sleep for too long."

Assessing the Cavalry mounts before them, Holton watches their glistening and salt-streaked flanks trotting at a steady clip. The mounted soldiers are much looser in their ranks and demeanor than when they rode out from the fort a week ago. Holton looks down at his Indian pony and gives it a pat on the neck. "Those mounts won't outlast the Apache for long in a running fight."

Holton and Denny acknowledge their predicament as they continue to follow the Cavalry troop. They both look back to the dog following in their tracks when he lets out a warning bark and a growl.

"What is it, Dog?" asks Holton.

Simultaneously, Denny and Holton see Stalking Wolf and his band of Apache descend from the rocks. The mounted Apache party unfurls from the rocks like a scorpion reaching out to strike. Holton and Denny spur their horses and ride up to Captain Parker. Denny gets there first and hollers over the clang of tack and gear, "Best give some quick orders, Capt'n!"

Captain Parker turns in the saddle and looks to the aggressing Apache. The company's line becomes sloppy as troopers spin in the saddle, hearing the bone-chilling war screams of the attacking Indians. Captain Parker raises his hand and hollers above the commotion, "Sergeant! Dismount and form a defensive line!"

Keeping hold of his mount as it dances around franticly, Holton yells to Parker and the sergeant, "Be sure to protect the horses or we'll have Apache upon us ten times over shortly."

The sergeant dismounts and hands off his horse. The cavalry troopers dismount with rifle in hand, and every fourth man takes hold of the horses. The sergeant bellows orders through the actions: "Take all measures to protect the horses!"

The Apache descend on the cavalry position while the soldiers form a line of defense with rifles ready. Holton and Denny remain astride their mounts and aim their rifles over the heads of the troopers. Captain Parker waits until the Apache are actually upon them and waves his arm through the air. "FIRE!"

Several Apache fall from their horses as the horseback warriors cut through the lines and circle around to approach on the flank. Captain Parker watches the action from his mount and yells to his troops.

"Every second man, reassemble on the flank!" The troopers shuffle and reload as the Apache split their ranks and circle the small company of blue coats.

Levering his rifle, Holton snaps off several shots. Denny takes a shot and lowers his rifle while looking around desperately. He yells over to Holton, "They're going to try to hold us here!"

Looking to the cloud of warring Apache approaching in the distance, Holton pulls cartridges from his gun belt and reloads. "Tell your captain that we need to get mounted, move out, and keep moving."

Spurring his horse, Denny circles around the troopers' line of defense and rides over to Captain Parker. The captain holds his saber high and fires off shots with his pistol.

The Apache circle and dive in toward the defensive line. Each time, they wound soldiers while taking casualties themselves. The thick, choking dust and war screams from the hostiles creates a sense of panicked survival for the Cavalry troops. The company of soldiers attempts to reassemble defensives and protect their mounts as the Apache constantly barrage them from horseback.

Denny steers his horse to Captain Parker and comes in extremely close, nearly ramming him from the saddle. "Sir, if we stay here much longer, it will be to the last man!"

Captain Parker regains his seat, takes aim, and fires his sidearm. "Your opinion is noted. They are getting the worst of it."

"It's only a trick to buy time." Denny points to the approaching mass of riders looming in the rocks to the distant horizon.

Captain Parker's jaw drops with the telling outcome of so many Apache upon them. He quickly considers his options when the blast of a bugle call echoes across the valley, and a volley of shots thunders from outside the defensive circle.

A company of Cavalry charges from the rocks to the south with Bear riding near the point. With Cavalry horses stretched out at full gallop they cover the distance to the engagement in short time. Thundering hooves and guidon flag high, their sidearms blaze lethal lead at the attacking warriors. Several Apache braves flee to the nearby rock outcroppings as Bear and the US Cavalry charge straight into the skirmish.

With obvious relief, Captain Parker reloads his pistol and looks on to the reinforcements.

"How did they find us? I say . . . someone has been saying their prayers!"

Denny laughs and draws his sidearm. "I'll be damned, it's ol' Bear!"

Several Apache are shot from their horses as the tide momentarily turns to the US Cavalry's advantage. Above the chaos, Apache orders are given as Stalking Wolf screams to his remaining braves. "Gather to the rocks to rejoin with the others!"

Through the commotion and gunfire, Holton hears Stalking Wolf's commanding screams and wheels his horse in that direction. A strange blinding compulsion takes over Holton as he pushes his way through the action toward his nemesis.

Stalking Wolf sees Holton fighting his way toward him and gives a nasty sneer. He touches the scar across his face and prods his horse toward the shelter of the rocks. Looking over his shoulder, he fires a shot toward Holton with his rifle. In a cloud of dust and men on war ponies, the Apache temporarily retreat into the rocky landscape.

The reinforcements surround and defend the troopers as Captain Parker orders his men to reassemble. Bear spots Holton at the fringe of the fighting as he breaks from the group in pursuit of the Apache riders. When he sees Holton's intention of riding after the Apache alone, he bellows out from the depth of his lungs with everything he's got, "Holton Lang!!"

Pulling up his mount suddenly, Holton glances back at the Cavalry troopers. He recognizes the emotional forces pushing him and ponders as he looks over at the ever-nearing dust cloud in the distance. He holds back and watches as the Apache attackers disappear into the rocks. Deterred from his retribution, he wheels his horse around and rides back toward the Cavalry position.

Easing his mount up next to Captain Parker, Bear takes his hat off and wipes the dust from his eyes with his neckerchief. "Capt'n, you had a mess of Apache behind that there rock who was jest 'bout to flank you."

Denny exchanges a knowing look with Bear. Captain Parker looks around and assesses his men, then gives a weak salute. "Good you came along when you did then, Mr. Benton."

Turning to his sergeant, Captain Parker again scans over his troopers and tries to regain his broken composure. "Sergeant, get everyone mounted and the wounded secured. We need to be moving out of here on the double."

"Yes, Sir!"

Knowing the lack of gratitude merely masks the officer's insecurity, Bear gives a shrug and looks to Denny with a bearded and toothy smile. "No thanks necessary, Capt'n . . . 'eh Denny, you led these troopers awful far in, don't ya think?"

The two Cavalry scouts drift away from the mounted officers while still watching their surroundings. Denny glances back at Captain Parker and looks to Bear. "Jest followin' their orders."

"These young officers sure ain't got a lick of sense when it comes to Apache. We tracked you for three days and weren't sure what we'd find."

The soldiers help the wounded get mounted, and some double up with the severely injured. Several bodies are merely draped over saddles and secured, as they didn't make it through the short, bloody skirmish.

Riding up to Bear and Denny, Holton halts his horse and sees Bear looking him over, concerned. He gives a shrug as he nods at Denny then lets a pained smile escape toward Bear.

"Bear . . . don't even ask."

"Thought I'd left you planted fer good in Arizona."

"I thought you had, too."

"Was Stalking Wolf, eh?"

Holton nods and watches the fight-torn soldiers get mounted and the wounded horses being dispatched. Bear follows his gaze to the Apache laden rocks and rubs his whiskers.

"There will be another time for that, Holton. We got to get these pups out of these hills if they're gonna live to fight another day."

Holton shakes off the obsession for Stalking Wolf and slides his rifle in the saddle scabbard. "Alright, let's get 'em out of here."

They look around to see that everyone is nearly mounted. Captain Parker rides to the front of the column and waves his arm. "Wounded to the front. Ho!"

With a clank and rattle, the merged companies of Cavalry move out. The ominous cloud of dust in the distance is on everyone's mind as they move out as quickly as possible without further injury to the already wounded.

Pulling out of the column to watch the troopers heading south, Bear turns his horse toward Holton. "What about that ranch of yours, and Charlie?"

Halting his horse, Holton backs him next to Bear. "Charlie has passed."

Removing his hat, Bear lowers his eyes for a moment. "He was a good sort of fella. Did he ask ya to leave the ranch 'nd come back here?"

"In his way, he did."

Bear spits a wad of chaw to the ground and wipes his whiskers. "What ya gonna do with it?"

"The land will still be there." Looking out to the distance, Holton watches for Apache. "I have something to attend to here yet."

Putting his hat back on, Bear looks to the spot where Stalking Wolf and the rest disappeared into the rocks. "You'll get a better chance at 'em."

"Maybe."

They watch the troopers trot past, and Bear scratches his neck. He looks at the sweaty grit and trail dust under his fingernails and wipes them on his shirt. "Ol' Charlie Nichols . . . he was a good pal. Hell, he managed that ranch near blind for who knows how long. Should hold out okay and not be too much worse for wear when you get back to it."

With a hint of a smile, Holton glances at Bear. "Yep, was Charlie's sentiments 'xactly."

"He was a wise old coot."

"You bet . . . was a good man."

Bear spits over his shoulder and wipes his whiskers. "First we got to get these soldier boys out of this valley."

Holton and Bear give their mounts a prod, and they fall in step with the column of Cavalry.

Chapter 33

The heat of midday comes on, and the troopers begin to ache in their necks from stealing glances over their shoulder and the fast trotting pace. Sun bleached and choked with sand, the wounded grit and grind their teeth on their neckerchiefs to keep from crying out from the uncomfortable but necessary retreat.

Following to the rear, Holton and Bear hang back from the dust of the soldiers' trail. Bear cuts a plug of tobacco and chews it before pushing it into his cheek. "Did you hear of their plan?"

Slightly amused, Holton acknowledges.

"Was it yer idea to draw the Apache out of the mountains?"

Bear wipes the whiskers under his lip and grins. "Yup, seemed like a good idea at the time."

Holton nods over his shoulder. "Well, they're a comin'."

"Yup."

They sit in a mutual silence for a time, letting the Cavalry gain some distance. With a knowing eye, Bear looks over Holton's roughened state. "You run into hard times of late?"

"I've had some Apache hospitality."

"Well, you look like hell."

"Feels worse on the inside."

With a grunt, Bear eases his horse to a walk, and Holton rides up beside. They ride along following the column of soldiers until Bear glances over his shoulder questioningly. "How many are there ya think?"

"As many as we have here, five times over."

Scratching his beard, Bear gives a whistle. "I guess we're going for broke."

"You bet."

Leading the large band of warriors to a vantage point, Malfonte looks over the two small companies of blue coats ahead. He watches menacingly and begins to tremble with the foreboding of violence. With a blood-curdling war whoop, the Apache chief charges forward, leading the hundreds of braves and war ponies toward the thin column of US Cavalry.

At the rear of the procession, Holton and Bear look behind to see the charging horseback Apache. Bear hooks his finger into his mouth to pull his chaw, and Holton gives him a slap on his dusty buckskin-clad back. "Well Bear, this is it!"

Bear tosses the wad of chaw aside and wipes his mouth. "Good knowin' ya, Holton."

Pulling his rifle from the saddle scabbard, Holton levers a round. "We ain't in the ground yet."

They jab spurs to their mounts, and with a flying leap to a gallop, they ride toward the troopers. Bear pulls to a sliding stop next to Captain Parker on his fired-up horse and hollers:

"There's two hundred Apache about to be upon us! Blow yer horn and get 'em moving!"

Waving his arm and barking commands at his sergeant, Captain Parker signals a retreat. At the sign of commotion, the disciplined troopers pull their ranks together, awaiting their orders. With a crisp bugle call, the whole column in unison breaks into a fleeing gallop.

In the wide-open high desert terrain, forty US Cavalry troopers move out at a full gallop pursued by two hundred screaming Apache. The gap between the two charging groups slowly closes, and both sides fire shots. The hundreds of pursuing Apache seem to be a specter of death, fanned out and half concealed by the trailing dust of the Cavalry.

Nearing the rocks that represent the informal entrance to the Guadalupe Mountains, the two horseback entities merge. The Cavalry and Indians ride as one mass body, fighting like a cancer from within. Soldiers along with Apache braves fall from their horses with a bloody mix of wounds as the running battle ensues. The choking dust, gunshots, and combination of blue coats and breechcloths make for a confusing and hectic arena.

Riding with his reins in his left hand and the big loop Winchester in his right, Holton rides full tilt in the fusion of battle. Twirl-cocking the rifle with one hand, Holton fires on the enemy as they ride near to him.

Holton steers his horse toward Bear when he sees a large Apache warrior ride up on his friend with his lance ready to plunge. The Apache draws back for the killing thrust on Bear as Holton spins another cartridge round into the chamber and extends the long firearm one-handed. Another Apache with a bladed war club rides across Holton's path and swings out toward a Cavalry rider. Holton hurriedly snaps off a shot and drops the Apache and his club from his racing pony.

Turning in the saddle, Bear is nearly face to face with the large, hostile Apache and his deadly lance. Bear aims his revolver, only to hear the deafening *click* of an empty chamber above the din of battle. The Apache, about to thrust the lance, suddenly jilts from a lethal gunshot and falls from his horse into the melee.

Bear looks back at Holton, giving a knowing shrug. They exchange a look of indebted friendship as Holton peels away into the fighting. Quickly, Bear pulls cartridges from his belt and reloads his pistol while still moving at a full gallop. He snaps the load gate of his single action revolver closed, swings the barrel out, and pistol whips an Apache that rides up next to him. The dazed warrior tumbles from his saddle, and Bear resumes combat.

The assembly of fighting men astride horse and pony emerges from the rocks and is met by the loud and distinct bugle charge of another column of US Cavalry. Riding in the lead, Lieutenant Colonel Merritt raises his sabre and charges with another two companies of Cavalry. They cover the terrain from the east and slam into the fighting mass of soldier and Apache. Horses and riders are pushed to the west as Merritt's blue-coated troopers charge into the fight.

Horses scream with fright and confusion as the two groups collide. Rearing and spinning, Malfonte holds on to his panicked war pony in the wave of oncoming soldiers. A shot tears into his chest, and he fires his gun and lets out his last battle wail. Another shot slams into his skull, and he tumbles to the ground in a motionless heap.

The running battle continues to the west as small groups of Apache try to break off and flee to the rocks of the Guadalupe Mountains. Over the thundering sound of hooves, orders are hollered, and troopers are diverted in all directions to gather and keep the Apache from dispersing. The running battle begins to take on more the form of a runaway stampede than a fight as the troopers try to keep the Apache corralled.

With Apache and soldiers all around, Holton reloads and chooses his hostile targets carefully while still at a full gallop. The running battle is a constant blur of flaying hooves, horsehide, dust, and gunshots. Holton cocks his rifle again and takes aim.

Suddenly, a lance is smashed across Holton's shoulders, and he is nearly knocked from his galloping horse. He recovers to see Stalking Wolf glaring over at him as he veers off to the north and the safety of the mountain rocks.

Rifle still in hand, Holton regains his seat in the saddle and charges after Stalking Wolf. He weaves his way through the mass of fighting men and rides hard trying to overtake the fleeing Apache before he reaches the rocks. Snapping off a shot, Holton spin cocks his rifle again while in pursuit.

Still in the thick of the fighting, Bear rides near Captain Parker as both watch Holton charge from the flow of battle. Captain Parker bristles at the thought of Holton making chase of what seems to be one lone Apache. Riding at a charging run, Captain Parker turns to several troopers fighting nearby and yells while pointing toward Holton, "Stop that man!"

Continuing to fire his pistol, Bear careens up alongside Captain Parker and blocks the cavalry troopers from their orders. "Let 'im go. That's Stalking Wolf he's after. Anyone else following an Apache into the rocks wouldn't have a chance."

The battle continues to cover ground west to the Bravo River as Holton follows Stalking Wolf into the rocky foothills and mountains. At the fringe of the running battle, Dog splits from the group and follows Holton's trail into the deadly rocks.

Chapter 34

The hostile terrain of the Guadalupe Mountains rises up and forms abruptly at the edge of the high desert landscape. Large rocks and boulders mark the entrance to the mountainous regions above. Filled with all types of wildlife, the majority of the foothills is able to be navigated by horseback. Several animal trails can be seen cutting to the upper elevations.

Riding into the rocks trailing Stalking Wolf, Holton follows the fresh hoof marks on the sandy ground. He moves deeper into the rocks until he gets to a cluster of boulders where the tracks disappear. Holton scans the rocks and trail for any sign of horse or rider. Steering his mount up through some boulders, he follows a narrow animal trail leading to higher ground.

Cresting the top of the gap, Holton looks around cautiously and listens into the coming wind. He momentarily keeps his breath as the hairs on the back of his neck prickle and rise with impending danger. Suddenly, he catches the faint and malevolent smell of blood in the breeze.

In a split second, as Holton turns his head, Stalking Wolf leaps from cover and is upon him. He tears Holton from the saddle, and they both tumble down the rocks to a stone ledge below the trail. Moving quickly in a flurry of limbs, they untangle from each other and simultaneously scurry to their feet. Stalking Wolf faces off and sneers at Holton. "You are the fool who follows an Apache into the rocks?"

"Know that I will chase you into hell."

They both catch their breath, and Stalking Wolf smiles wickedly. "You finally come to find your death, half blood?"

Filling with rage, knowing this is the moment he has been yearning for, Holton spits his words at Stalking Wolf in Apache: "This day is your last, Stalking Wolf."

As the two circle each other, Stalking Wolf draws a knife, and Holton follows suit with his own blade. "I will lay you down like I did your squaw," growls Stalking Wolf.

In a fit of fury, Holton lunges and is deflected by Stalking Wolf as their blades meet. Stalking Wolf deftly thrusts his knife and slashes Holton across the neck. Reeling back, Holton tries to regain his composure and not let his anger push him into the attacking blade. He touches the trace of blood from his slight neck wound and continues the circling standoff. Stalking Wolf watches Holton bleed and laughs. "I will cut out your eyes and hang them from my horse."

With a wave of his knife, Holton motions to the ugly scar that serves as a distinct divider between the two halves of Stalking Wolf's face. "I have come to finish what I had begun, you two-faced liar and killer of women and old men."

Stalking Wolf guffaws and twirls his knife. "I did that old man a favor. Apache warriors should not live to be such an age. They become weak like old squaws . . ."

An evil sneer knowingly tickles Stalking Wolf's features as he continues to bait Holton.

". . . and old squaws, your woman begged for me to take her like a full Apache."

Holton chokes back his anger and emotions and attempts to turn his feelings into a verbal attack on Stalking Wolf. "She said you had your braves do what you could not. You hide behind fighting men like a child in a storm."

Angered, Stalking Wolf's scar scrunches into a zig-zag of flesh like a lightning bolt full of venom. He fakes a lunge to one side, then charges his weapon into Holton.

Knife blades clank and glisten as the two entangle and slam to the ground. They roll across the rock, desperately trying to get the upper hand. Grunts of survival erupt from the fight as they stab and gouge at each other.

In a swift and deft move, Stalking Wolf gets the advantage in the bout. He clasps on to Holton's back and jerks his knife blade up to the base of his prey's neck. Holton quickly grabs hold of the blade and keeps it from slicing into his jugular. The bloodied Apache hunting blade shakes at Holton's throat with Stalking Wolf's hand of death hovering between the pushing and pulling forces.

Slowly, the blade presses into Holton's flesh, and an evil smile creeps across Stalking Wolf's physically strained features. The pain from the sharp edge of the blade biting into his neck gives Holton renewed strength. The two continue their standoff, trembling with exertion.

The still air surrounding them becomes void of all sound other than their gasping breath as they struggle in their battle of redemption. Finally, Holton's energy begins to wane, and the knife blade creeps in and presses into his neck again. He lets out a slow gasp with his final efforts.

The silence is broken with a growl and a snap of teeth. Dog leaps from the rocks and latches onto Stalking Wolf's shoulder. Screaming with the shock and pain of the canine's bite, Stalking Wolf releases his grip on the blade at Holton's throat.

Reeling in pain, Stalking Wolf reaches back to detach the jaws of sharp teeth from the muscle in his shoulder. Taking firm hold of the dog's neck and scruff, he tries to tear him loose from his bite.

As the attacking knife blade clanks to the rocks, Holton follows it to the ground in a heap. He rolls and looks up at Stalking Wolf and Dog in violent engagement. Screaming in anguish, Stalking Wolf finally tears Dog free from his biting grip and hurls him against the rocks. Quickly, he turns back to Holton, takes two steps, and leaps onto him.

The yelp of dog hitting the rocks masks the agonizing and death-telling groan of Stalking Wolf. The scar on his face shows with painful surprise the feeling of Holton's knife thrust deep in his chest. Rolling free, Stalking Wolf disbelievingly looks down to see the blade of Holton's knife buried to the hilt.

Kneeling next to Stalking Wolf, Holton takes hold again of the knife handle and stares into his enemy's eyes. He whispers in cold, deliberate Apache tongue, "You took Miryan . . . my life, from me."

Stalking Wolf glares up at Holton with a fierce, unrepentant stare. Pressing down, Holton twists the fatal blade deeper into Stalking Wolf's chest. He squirms silently like a snake underfoot as Holton pushes the knife blade through him. With a swift uppercut to his heart, Holton holds the knife firm as Stalking Wolf arches into death. "Now I take everything from you!"

His anger finally quelled, Holton pulls the knife from Stalking Wolf's chest. He stands and looks down at the still body of the dead Apache warrior. Heaving for breath, he stares a long time as the image of revenge slowly soothes his deep-seated memories of loss.

Finally at a sort of peace, Holton bends down next to Stalking Wolf's body and scans the rocky terrain of the surrounding mountains. With a whimper, Dog crawls over and lies at Holton's feet. Holton looks down at the mongrel dog and sinks down to his haunches next to him.

The quiet sounds of nature return with the warm breeze off the dry mountains. Pained and fatigued, Holton eases back into the shade of the rocks and lies down. He stares at the lifeless body of Stalking Wolf a long while, then looks up to the clear blue sky. Holton nods at Dog as he curls nearby, and with a slight gasp of breath, he slips into an exhausted slumber.

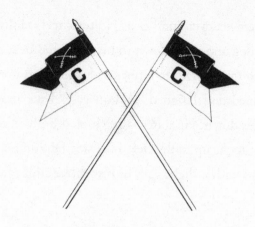

Chapter 35

The Bravo River runs clear and fast near the watershed of the mountains. The battle is over, and the remaining hostile Apache are led horseback under guard of the US Cavalry. The afternoon heat has quelled, and the battle-weary look shows on all faces, Apache and soldier.

Riding along the banks of the Rio Bravo, Holton travels at an easy lope horseback, followed by the dog. He rides past Lieutenant Colonel Merritt, to whom he gives a nodding salute and receives one in return. Bear separates from the slow-moving mass and rides out to meet Holton. The two ease their hard-ridden and lather-crusted horses up next to one another.

"You know somthin' Holton . . . I lose a bet every time you show up again."

"You never was good at wagering."

Holton smiles at Bear, then looks around at the group of wounded and battle-worn Apache. The smile falls from his face as he senses the end of a proud and honorable fighting people. Bear rides alongside him and notices his change in mood.

"Malfonte is dead somewheres back there, and these Mescalero are finished with their raiding parties on West Texas. Jest clean-up and reservation assignments now."

Shaking his head sadly, Holton looks out over the wide, shallow river. "The waters will keep rolling on."

Bear nods. "And it washes away most wounds."

Holton looks to Bear, and they exchange a familiar and longstanding look of friendship.

"Marks the end of another life," Holton muses.

Bear looks out over the procession. "For them and you."

They both ride quietly for a while. Holton looks down at the dog following and touches his neckerchief to the bloody wound on his neck. "Seems like a lifetime ago."

Looking from Holton's near-fatal neck wound to the dog following in their trail, Bear laughs one of his raucous belly laughs. "Yup. Least you got that ugly dog to spend your time with now. Must be yer cookin' that keeps him around."

Glancing down at the dog, Holton praises him with his eyes as Dog looks up and wags his tail. "Not much to look at, but good to the core."

Thinking a moment, then smiling at Bear, Holton laughs. "Like someone else I know."

Bear eyes Holton sidelong, rubs his chin whiskers, and winces. "I ain't that much . . ."

He looks down at the mongrel dog and sniffs, ". . . or that ugly."

The afternoon sun nears the horizon and casts an orange and purple hue on the marching troopers. Holton and Bear ride shoulder to shoulder alongside one another. Watching Dog run off after a meal of jackrabbit, Holton looks over to Bear. "What's next for you, Bear?"

Pulling and scratching his coarse whiskers, Bear pauses and thinks. "I was thinking 'bout heading west to Arizona again. There's gold up in them Chiricahua Mountains."

Holton gives Bear an amused glance. "You ain't up for ranchin'?"

"Not hardly."

The rhythmic jangle of marching horses in the US Cavalry drowns out the sounds of the wind blowing through the scrub trees. The Apache prisoners walk with their heads held proud, knowing their final days of warrior existence. The sounds of man and horse seem to blend with the rushing river noise as the procession continues.

The setting sun glows brilliant on the West Texas landscapes as the two friends, Holton and Bear, separate from the military column and continue to ride along. Into the west, two rode together.

The End